Praise for Death is a Hungry Angel

"This beautifully written slow burn of a novel is like a masterclass in character development."

Pierre C. Arseneault, author of *Maple Springs* and *Something Happened in Carlton*

Other Books by Leah Holbrook Sackett

Swimming Middle River
White Knight Escort Service
Raising St. Elisabeth
You Don't Know Who You Are Until You've Gone Too Far
Catawampus in Sweetgum County

DEATH IS A HUNGRY ANGEL

Leah Holbrook Sackett

ISBN: 978-1-963832-37-2 (paperback)
ISBN: 978-1-963832-52-5 (ebook)
LCCN: 2025944493

Shadow Dragon Press
9 Mockingbird Hill Rd
Tijeras, New Mexico 87059
www.shadowdragonpress.com
info@shadowdragonpress.com

Content Notice: This book includes the death of a loved one, traumatic guilt, attacks by paranormal forces, dealing with grief and loss, and a lot of other bad stuff. There is also the unfortunate death of a family pet.

For Michael
With a special thanks to Io, River, and Jonathan.

Contents

Prologue

Wade Family Death Hospital and Funeral Home

1918

Beverly

THERE WILL BE A funeral this week.

Mr. Jeffries died last night at his dinner table in front of his wife and two children. This is what I overheard from Mrs. Jeffries as she made the funeral plans with my grandma in the front parlor.

Their dinner table had almost been set to Mr. Jeffries's liking. His eldest child, Mary, set the table as usual but she was distracted by her new ginger tabby cat, Mr. Mischief, who liked to snag the ankles of her school socks in a playful fashion as she worked about the wobbly table with mismatched chairs. Everything in the Jeffries' house was recovering from or waiting to be smashed by Mr. Jeffries's anger.

Mary had wanted a cat forever but had no hopes of getting one until last week. Unexpectedly, Mr. Jeffries said yes to the cat that showed up at the front door with a dead mouse dangling from its mouth. It had made a smart and compelling argument for itself. Although small, a dead baby mouse screamed the potential horrors of disease. And Mary pointed out that Mr. Mischief looked cuddly despite the death offering.

"The cat may be worth it, if he keeps the place clear of mice," Mary's mother said to Mr. Jeffries.

This was a rare moment when Mrs. Jeffries made an argument on her children's behalf. She spoke without looking up at Mr. Jeffries. She never did look Mr. Jeffries in the eye anymore. He trained her to always watch his fists. At the moment of the cat request, Mrs. Jeffries was proud to take a stand for her daughter. But deep down, her fear of mice was the real motivator.

She recently caught her index finger in one of the mouse traps tucked in the corners of the pantry. She didn't dare call Dr. Craggenmore and waste money on a finger. But after a week with a homemade splint, it looked like it would heal crooked. Mrs. Jeffries's looks had been beaten out of her long ago, so what did one finger matter? But it did.

Due to the cat's frivolity, on the night of Mr. Jeffries's demise, Mary mistakenly placed the saltshaker next to her younger brother's plate.

"Children, come to dinner," their mother called.

Everyone spoke softly and moved with care in the Jeffries' house, except Mr. Jeffries. His violent and loud outbursts were frequent and yet hard to predict. He seated himself at the head of the table with a terrible glare cast over the supper and his family.

Mr. Jeffries had another headache that day. He'd seen Dr. Craggenmore earlier in the week. But according to Mr. Jeffries, "That quack hadn't done a goddamn thing."

At least, that's what I heard from his youngest child, Simon, who came with his mother to our front parlor.

According to Mrs. Jeffries, during spring planting and harvest time each year, Mr. Jeffries was beset with raging headaches. He begrudged Simon's easy school day of sitting indoors and looking at useless books. The only book the Jeffries owned was the Bible. And even with that, you'd never catch Mr. Jeffries reading it due to his lack of interest in anything scholarly. Despite Mr. Jeffries's refusal to read, it didn't stop him from knowing everything in that Bible, or so he said. And it made him some kind of judgmental authority. Lording the Lord over anyone smaller than him.

What Mr. Jeffries wanted was a son to work the fields, not to read books, even if it was the Bible. But Simon's mother had protested for one more year in the schoolhouse. The boy was too young yet for the field, and besides, his learnin' would come in handy with keeping the farm books. According to the headmaster at the local school, little Simon was already showing a knack for numbers.

I know he had a real knack for marbles, so this is probably true.

"Simon will grow into a helpful lad," Mrs. Jeffries said to Mr. Jeffries, begging more time for her young son before he was burdened with the full wrath of Mr. Jeffries out in the field. Out in Mr. Jeffries' dominion, where she could do nothing to shield Simon from the hardships of working the soil or the sunbeaten brutality of his father. Small Simon would be ruined. All of his little boy softness hammered out of him. Mrs. Jeffries had fought for what limited protection she could offer her young son.

On the other hand, Mary was somewhat guarded in the sphere of domestic duties, which meant she was also of little use to Mr. Jeffries, being a girl and all. Whereas she was a great help to Mrs. Jeffries around the house. Mr. Jeffries often expressed how tired he was of being the only one to pull his weight in this family.

The night he died, still wearing his manure-caked boots at the dinner table, it was Mr. Jeffries's privilege to say Grace. "We give thanks, our Lord, for the food I have worked so hard to provide for this family. May we all know our place and give thanks."

Mr. Jeffries took three thick slices of meatloaf from the chipped blue platter. Then he helped himself to half the bowl of mashed potatoes before passing the remaining food for the rest of his family to take part. Mr. Jeffries loved mashed potatoes. So did Simon; it was one of the few things they had in common.

Mr. Jeffries reached out for the saltshaker, but there was only the pepper shaker, and he unwittingly over-peppered his meal. When he realized his mistake, he slammed his fists on the table.

"Where is the salt? Why is it by Simon's plate? Mary, look what you did. This is all your fault, girl," Mr. Jeffries hollered. Spit flew from his lips and landed on Mary's cheek, rough with psoriasis. Dr. Craggenmore couldn't do much for her psoriasis either.

"Boy, hand me that salt. You stupid fool," Mr. Jeffries bellowed.

I imagined he was allowing himself to work up into a frenzy. He might even have swatted his son down in shame to teach him a lesson. But instead, he was struck with a pain in his chest and, mid-barrage of impolite slurs, he gave off and clutched at his heart. His puffed-up anger and superiority gave way to shock.

And then he landed face first in his peppery mashed potatoes and meatloaf.

I am tucked behind the parlor curtains, an enormous swathe of burgundy velvet, to catch a glimpse of the grieving family and listen to what is said between the women. What I see is Simon's dry eye, and Simon's older sister, Mary, has the left side of her face buried in her mother's arm. Her pose looks like one of grief, but everyone in the parlor knows better. The psoriasis makes her shy.

Outside his mother and sister's embrace, Simon finally notices me hiding behind the curtains that keep knocking the big blue bow on my curls askew, and he decides to join me in the heavy folds. I am glad for the company behind the parlor curtains, which Grandma insists is a luxury for the dead. Grandpa thinks it has more to do with vanity.

"Death is a dirty business," Grandma liked to say while scrubbing, washing, and dressing the dead. "And it's the Wades's job to clean it up and make it presentable."

Grandma takes her role seriously as mistress of this house for the dead. She works tirelessly to put out all the personal touches that made death a thing of beauty.

Even though I am just a little girl of seven, I am not too young to learn the traditions and sanctity of a proper burial. Even if a great part of that education comes from being seen and not heard. Or not even seen. There is a good deal to learn from adults when they think no one is listening.

There is something about death that makes confession good for the soul of the survivors. I hung on her every word as Mrs. Jeffries unburdened herself to Grandma. Since I live in a death hospital and funeral home, my understanding of life is steeped in death. I sometimes wonder what I would learn listening to a different household, one centered on life.

Whispering in the velvet folds with Simon, I learn the finer points of Mr. Jeffries's demise. Initially, I thought the Jeffries family would be relieved, but things aren't that simple. Mr. Jeffries was the one who put food on the table.

"It's all my fault," Simon whispers to me.

"How?" I ask while setting that floppy blue bow straight.

"Just as he was hollerin' at me, I wished under my breath that he were dead. I've wished that a hundred times, but this time he actually died. It was obvious how his face plopped into the mashed potatoes nose deep. No one could breathe like that."

"Are you magic?" I ask.

"I guess so, or at least last night I was."

Simon is petrified by the power of his wishes, but he wouldn't wish his father back to life. Not even for more mashed potatoes.

"I'm not sorry," Simon says. "It did bother me a little to wish my own father dead, but it bothered me more to see those mashed potatoes wasted."

I could see the shadow of fear on Simon's face. It isn't grief. It is fear of his father returning for vengeance.

"The dead don't come back. You are safe," I say with confidence and reach out to hold his chubby, clammy hand just like I'd seen Grandma do with the grieving.

Grandma is a toucher, a comforter. She's always patting and hugging at the right moment. I want to be just like her. Simon's dirty little hand leaves a mark on the skirt of my white sailor dress, but I don't mind—even though I know Grandma will mind later. I pat the grubby hand with comfort and conviction.

I know my words to be true because Samael is in the death chamber with Mr. Jeffries right now.

Chapter 1
Welcome to Wade House

Wade House

2021

Anna

The three of us are living under an unspoken rule of no happy thoughts allowed. There is no safety, no forgiveness in a world without my little sister.

Dad's mistake hangs in wet patches on his chest and armpits of his favorite gray t-shirt. The day isn't even hot enough for sweat yet, but the warmth of the morning predicts an unwanted heat wave. Perspiration beads up on Dad's brow. He's blundered, and he knows it. We know it. But he isn't going to own it. He isn't even going to see things through. He will be leaving us for a business trip with his new job the day after tomorrow. Heck, Dad isn't even going to be around long enough to help Mom and me unpack. He grips the steering wheel like his life depends on his belief in this move.

"It is just what the family needs," he declares for the millionth time. He wraps his fists tighter around the steering wheel, enough that it starts to shimmy.

It's been six months since the accident. Not one of us can believe six months has already passed.

I woke early every day since my sister, Abby, died. I hated waking early to the bitter roast of my mother's black coffee wafting from her perch in the doorway to Abby's room and snagging on my empty stomach. Mom's haggard face told the tale of too little sleep and too much crying. Dad would linger a foot behind her at all times. Like he was ready to catch her—but I knew she'd already fallen.

Bathed in the soft morning light, the sunshine played on her shadowed features and amplified the longing and loss etched on her face. Still, she was beautiful. She was a picture of what Abby would never grow up to be. I pulled the blankets over my head and sensed it was wrong to think that way.

Mom stood waiting, watching over the room, just the same as Abby left it. Abby was always the neat sister. Her bed, carefully made, and her schoolbooks neatly stacked on her little white wooden desk froze the room in time. The elementary school requested Abby's books be returned numerous times, but Mom deleted the messages. Outside of the white furniture, pink dominated the room.

Abby was seven when she passed away. And none of us knew how to move on.

The day Dad tracked his cell to inside the fridge and then his car keys under a six-deep pile of pizza boxes—a concerning cockroach hotel—he realized he had to do something. On impulse, Dad purchased this house sight unseen. "A fantastic steal: a big, old white wood-framed house with eight large rooms and one and a half bathrooms," he said in feigned excitement. While the house is bigger than what we need, two full baths would have been nice.

Dad is determined the family will make the best of things. Get back on track. Start anew. And any other Pollyanna sentiment he can think of, which make my insides squirm like I swallowed a bucket of worms.

We make a slow roll up the cracked blacktop street, and the house gains in size as we approach. We creep up on the foreboding dump as though we might scare it. Then Dad stops at the beginning of the gravel drive, pockmarked with ruts and weeds. A perfect introduction to the overgrown and desiccated grounds that stretch back to a shaky-looking garage.

This! This is where he is moving us?

Dad shudders as he bears the hot glares of Mom and me. There is nowhere to hide.

Parched vegetation covers every inch of the property. The lawn is yellow; even the tall weeds are yellow. Everything about this place calls for a drink. I can tell by the look of concentration on Dad's face that he is worrying he won't remember which box his whisky has been packed in. We left in a mad rush, marking too many boxes as *MISC* or not marked at all. The remainder of our lives feels miscellaneous after Abby has gone. Dad's shaking hand reveals he really could use a drink right now. Instead, he frees his right hand from the steering wheel and chews his nails.

Biting his nails is one of his lesser quirks, which he has passed on to me. I always seem to get the lesser of everything. Nail chewing and quitting has become our father-daughter pastime.

Dad peers into the rearview mirror at me, the now-only daughter. My fourteen-year-old angular face glares back at him. I know he is looking back for Abby holding her teddy bear Georgie. I can tell by the smile on his face. But I have claimed Georgie as my own and my pointy chin buried into Georgie's plush head takes shape in the backseat. He cannot face me. He uses the mirror to glance back again, and even then, he immediately clamps his eyes shut and turns his head. The living daughter is a no-good thing to be.

My disheveled hair makes a curtain over my face, a greasy veil to peer out from and judge the world around me. This veil doubles as a fortress, keeping my parents from penetrating my little world. My default setting these days is an angry countenance aimed at blocking Mom and Dad from seeing my pain. However, Dad sees the pain all the same. The pain is everywhere he looks, and he can't fix any of it.

Parked in front of our new dump, I mean home, Mom and I bear the tell-tale signs of numbed mourners. We sit slack and small in our seats with a far-off gaze. We cower under the looming frown of the house. If asked, we would have agreed that we are arrived at another funeral. I clutch Georgie tighter. My awkward adolescent features contrast with Georgie's fluff, and I glower over the well-loved, pastel pink bear. I am no Abby for sure; even Georgie feels that.

Since the young age of three, Georgie belonged to Abby. He was her best friend for more than half her life. He was a birthday gift from a now-forgotten giver. Someone then well-thought-of enough to be a guest at a three-year-old's party. Someone now distant enough to be forgotten in the tightly bound years since.

At age seven, Abby had just begun to leave Georgie behind on her bed when she went to scouts or softball. Leaving Georgie at home was Abby's first declaration of independence, reluctant as it may have been. Inside the house, Georgie went everywhere with her.

He was tacky with food stains and snot marks. Mom waited for Abby to leave so she could wash Georgie. Clean as she might, he always carried the scent of Abby, a mix of animal crackers and cherry lip balm. Once, Mom stole him away for the laundry when Abby was sleeping, but Abby woke up to find Georgie missing. She stood on her bed, clutching a pink knit blanket, hysterically screaming for Georgie. Mom appeared in the doorway out of breath and with a semi-damp bear in hand. She didn't rewash Georgie until the day Abby went with her Girl Scout troop to sell surplus boxes of cookies. It was a doomed February Friday.

I sniff the top of Georgie's stuffed head, trying hard to find tones of Abby's scent buried under the mask of Tide detergent. Georgie was special in the way all truly loved toys are special; in the same way sisters are special. Georgie was privy to secrets and giggles. On the night of the burial, I claimed Georgie for myself, and I've never slept without him since. At first, Mom wanted to put him back on Abby's bed. But her grief for Abby made the slightest budge when she realized I needed the bear, and that was how Abby would have wanted it.

Everyone said the family needed a fresh start. *"A fresh start, a fresh start."* I would punch something if I heard that phrase again. I did not believe this worn-out cliché would solve all our problems. It promised a life without sorrow, which almost certainly was a lie. The phrase implied a life without Abby, and that was no life at all.

So, we left the hustle and bustle of St. Louis, a hubbub of suburban life, a lifestyle of the overcrowded and overbooked. We left the race to look like we had it all to land in another place where kids fall through the cracks. And by the size of the cracks in the road, that might be literal. To me, we are moving away from home, overexposed by Abby's absence, to a place where my parents can hide from their mourning. We arrive at a place where no one matters, especially me.

Mom and I step gingerly from the car's safety and onto the soft crush of gravel. The rocks shift under Mom's weight, much like the gentle give of our family's stability, of Mom's sanity. Mom shuts the car door softly as if trying not to wake the dead, except she does wish to wake the dead. She wants nothing more than to embrace what is just out of reach, out of the corner of her eye. Even here, in this place, Mom feels like Abby is on the fringe of coming home. I do not share her hope.

Already, Mom realizes we've escaped nothing. Death lurks among us. Mom stares at Dad while he fidgets on the sloping gray wooden slats of the front porch. No one wants to be the first person inside. Mom takes a deep breath and tries to hold it. This gasping for air has become an annoying habit ever since Abby's passing, as if holding her breath will keep Abby from fading away. I wonder why we ever left our home with Abby's touch everywhere. This move is a mistake.

Mom and I form a cautious line behind Dad. I still have Georgie clutched to my chest. The heavy lock in Dad's grasp reluctantly rolls over to grant access to the house, which is dark and choking for air. He fumbles in the poorly lit room for a light switch while Mom pulls the shades up. They are vinyl roller shades from the 1960s that roll up with a snap if you know how to tug them. The first shade Mom touches in the front window crashes to the hardwood floor, making us jump. I notice what appears to be a honey-toned natural wood flooring, but I can't tell for sure with the lack of light and the heavy blanket of dust.

I have the distinct sense that our presence, heck, our noise, has awakened something up from a long slumber. It yawns before us with all the menace of a haunted house.

Shit.

"Just imagine," Dad says. "We can make this house our own. Think how beautiful the floors will be once polished?" He extends his right leg like an olive branch and sweeps his shoe across the floor in an arc. This swish of his foot shoos away what I hope are healthy-sized dust bunnies, not dead mice.

Neither Mom nor I throw him a bone, and we turn toward the front door as if plotting an escape. But then we dutifully pivot to walk deeper into the house. Tightly formed, we work our way past the two spacious front rooms and find a mint-green tiled bathroom across the hall from a dark bedroom with bamboo shades. These shades are much more amiable to rolling up and reveal scattered sunshine through a filthy window. Another room, off the bedroom, is too dark to see and too small to be of much interest. Mom decides that's where Abby's boxes will be stored. Out of the way, yet close by.

The space tucked away in the shadows gives me the sensation of being watched, and my skin crawls just a bit. Mom wraps her arms around herself and chuffs her hands up and down to restore the warmth in her body.

How can it be cold with the quickly climbing temperature? It has to be at least 104 degrees inside this oven of a tomb.

Although it makes me uncomfortable, I turn my back on this dark place. But I do so with chagrin. I refuse to give in to the juvenile thought that a monster lurks in the dark. I follow Mom to resume the tour to the kitchen, a vast black-and-white expanse that manages not to feel like the warm hub of activity it is meant to be.

"Oh, you will do wonderful things here, uh, we will," Dad says, picking up the neck of his t-shirt and rubbing it against the bridge of his nose in a pointless gesture to blot the sweat.

Mom gives him a sidelong glance. While I inch my

way toward Dad, I begin to feel sorry for him. I can see the darkening sweat stains growing on his shirt and his rapid blinking, trying to keep the sweat out of his eyes. I remind myself that Dad must have dragged us out here with good intentions.

We wander about in the misdirected sunlight of the kitchen. The light breaks and warps through the glass block window, which does not open. It is a poor choice as the only window for such a vast room. Ventilation is limited to the small exhaust fan in the stove hood—if that even works. This fan is clearly an afterthought and a few decades late for the original kitchen.

The spacious kitchen has a deep porcelain sink and an old-fashioned stove with a griddle. It's a working kitchen with a wooden island at its heart. The scarred island had been well-worn in the distant past. It looks like the place one would make bread, a lot of bread. I decide the kitchen holds the most promise. Perhaps Dad and I could make his special oatmeal-everything cookies. But then again, maybe not. Mom and Dad have both refrained from engaging in old family traditions since the loss of Abby. I begin thinking I should be right there with Abby, dead.

We muddle through the house tour as a fractured unit, and finally, we come upon the sunroom. There are no shades here. Sixteen tall, narrow windows wrap the room, begging to be washed. Mom is drawn to the windows, but a look of disappointment graces her face. The windows offer a poor view of an overgrown yard choked by wilted prairie grass and weeds that stretch out before ending in a plot of huddled stones peeking around the back corner of the garage. In the center of these stones stands a majestic and craggy dead tree that might be considered lit looking when Halloween comes around.

Mom crosses to the left side of the room and presses her forehead against a window. "Oh, look, a peach tree with heavy boughs," she says.

From where I stand, I can't tell if the tree bears ripe fruit. From here, I can only see one peach among the branches. But it is a sign of life after all. Even with all the windows and on this sunny day, the room has a chilly presence, slowly giving up the fight against the heat of the day. Mom turns her back to the windows. She heeds some bid to move deeper inside the house. As do I.

"What's upstairs?" I ask.

"I don't know. Let's go find out, Anna Banana," Dad says.

"Daaad."

"Oh, sorry. I know. I know. You're not a baby anymore." He looks furtively at Georgie clutched to my chest.

Mom takes up the rear as we head back to the front of the house, seeking the staircase. Together we climb the moss green-colored carpeted stairs. We find one large bedroom facing the front of the house and one unfinished room at the back, identical in size. In between is a sitting area with a dusty, empty built-in bookcase, and off this space, a half bath.

"Every inch of this house needs work, not to mention to be thoroughly cleaned," Mom says. "And to be honest, I'm a little afraid the dirt and dust are what's holding this thing together."

"Honey, this old house has great bones. And we can update it," Dad says.

"Why can't I get service? Heck, I don't even have a signal," I say. I aggressively poke my phone with my stubby fingers. As I am a nail-biter like Dad, the stunted appearance of my fingers makes the exaggerated prodding appear all the clumsier. I desperately try to will the phone to find service but wishes never work out for me.

"I'll call the internet company, and I'll fix everything," Dad says.

I can read the grimace on his face. He's secretly thanking God for his upcoming business trip. The gleam generally found in his eyes has diminished since Abby died. Now, as he hopes he isn't lying, the weight of this doomed house makes the light in his eyes go out altogether.

Mom wanders into the front bedroom. "What's with this? The last owner left this behind?" she asks no one.

We all turn our attention to the massive polished chifforobe, a hulking piece of furniture with an odd beauty. In this filthy place, the glossy antique with a swirl of red rings and no hint of dust stands out. Why this enormous museum-quality hunk of furniture has been stashed away like a treasure in this sore thumb, this tomb of a house, is anyone's guess. Dad runs his hands over the dated yet still beautiful wood. He puts his shoulder and all his weight into shoving the chifforobe, but there is not the slightest shift. Mom tries to pull open the door, but it's locked or stuck shut.

I think it is perfectly placed in this room of slapdash renovations from the turn of the century to the 1960s, by the look of things. "Dibs! I call it. This is going to be my bedroom."

"Are you sure? This room reeks of cigarette smoke. Ugh," Mom says.

"I don't care. I want it."

"Well, seems like the chifforobe comes with the room," she says.

"That's fine. I'm beginning to think I like old stuff."

"Alright, that's my girl, Anna Banana," Dad says.

"Daaad."

"Oh, right, right," he says.

He shuffles his feet in his brown work boots over to where Mom stands. Dad must be proud of my bravery and hopes my newfound spunk will rub off on Mom. Heck, I think he hopes it will rub off on him.

"What do you think, Cynthia? You and I can take that room off the kitchen as our bedroom while I finish out this other room up here."

Mom rolls her eyes and gives a tight-lipped smile. A piece of blonde hair escapes the loose bun on the back of her head and brushes her cheek before tickling her collarbone. Mom brushes the strand back behind her ear. I watch my parents from over Georgie's head. I hear the weariness in Dad's voice mixed with hope. I can see the increasing boniness in Mom. For the first time since the funeral.

"Well, it's time to start unloading the U-Haul," Dad announces. "Big things first," he says, trying to control something.

I turn away from my parents to face the chifforobe and wrinkle my nose at the heavy stink of cigarettes. I bury my face in Georgie, hunting for the sugary scent of my sister.

Chapter 2

Death Cries for No One

Wade Family Death Hospital and Funeral Home

1918

Beverly

OUR HOUSE WAS ALWAYS an intimate operation of death. In the mid-1800s, my great-great-grandfather built this squat, white wooden framed house to serve as a family home and a place for wayward souls. By the early 1900s, my grandfather and father had renovated the upstairs attic space to expand the living quarters with the hopes of a growing family. All they got was me.

Wade Death Hospital and Funeral Home was a solemn and proud formality of tradition. The business side of death was conducted with wakes, hymnals, and mourners milling about flowers and mementos of the dearly departed. It was also my lively and lonely stomping grounds, as the only child of the Wades. I was different from other children. I was growing up in the ropey machinations of a death hospital. Some children had toys and games. I had corpses and Samael.

Wade House was where people ended up and were

turned out fit for the grave. The first floor was a tight-knit set of rooms, including the kitchen, a sixteen-window sunroom with a larger-than-necessary dining table, a roomy bathroom with large marble tiles of minty green, two small, conjoined bedrooms—one for my father and one for my grandparents—a living room, and the funeral parlor, which was the largest room in the house.

The funeral parlor functioned as a place for body display with any required pomp and circumstance for the deceased's family members or the more meager obligatory viewing of a John Doe by the town. Oddly, the John Does always have the biggest turnout. People liked to gawk at death when it wasn't one of their own. This front room also housed our Wade family Christmas tree.

This year's tree was well-spent, tipping, leaning against the wall, and shedding its needles. The dead Christmas tree was loosely wrapped in old newspapers to reduce the mess of pine needles. It was March, and Grandma could make no more excuses for its presence in the parlor. Ready to be discarded, the fragile leftover of a holiday waited its turn to be buried today, along with Mr. Jeffries.

My task was keeping the funeral parlor tidy, which was a challenge with all the fallen pine needles. I crawled about the parlor floor and collected the debris of crushed flowers amidst the pine needles. I wore my soft blue leather shoes with pearl buttons to protect my feet from the piercing pine needles, even though the size-too-small shoes pinched. The browning pine needles jutted up from the carpet of pale-yellow lilies backed by a tight crimson weave, a sneaky offensive on the part of the dead Christmas tree.

Everything that came to our house came to die. Except me. Even my father and grandparents showed the wear and tear of death about them.

I was glad to see both the Christmas tree and Mr. Jeffries go. The usual volunteer town pallbearers, who were also the volunteer fire brigade of six strong men, had removed Mr. Jeffries's casket and carried him to his final resting place in the graveyard. The Jeffries family followed behind for the graveside service. Afterward, my father discreetly dragged the prickly dead tree down to the cemetery. When all the people had gone, he'd tossed the shaky-limbed tree into the hole with Mr. Jeffries. A small brass bell still hung on the tree and tinkled with every dump of dirt shoveled upon it, as if it were ringing the last goodbye of Christmas hope.

The bell did not chime for Mr. Jeffries; he'd already been devoured by Samael.

Giving up my spying post at the gate of the cemetery, I hiked back up the long yard to the funeral parlor, where I collected odd items and canvassed the room, making it ready for the next wave of mourners. I had a clean-up process. First, I swept the room's perimeter, rubbing against the walls papered with a burgundy velvet-flocked baroque design. Next, I crawled between the diminutive red velvet-upholstered chairs that populated the room in rows and had been handmade by the older generations of our family. Occasionally, in the line of duty and play, I knelt upon a pine needle, which would prick my tender skin and draw a bead of blood. I was careful never to bleed on my white dress or anything else in the fancy parlor. I would apply pressure to the bead of blood with my thumb for a few minutes. Then I would suck my thumb clean and continue.

Despite the many chairs, people had plenty of space for milling about the floral funeral arrangements, the glass-encased hair wreaths on display, and the stretcher for the coffin. Hair wreaths fashioned from the cut hair of the deceased were a memento made by and for loved ones. Frequently, a hair wreath was commissioned from Grandma, renowned for her elegant designs and quick turnaround. Grandma was passing down this skill to me. I liked making hair wreaths; the hair strands slipped through my fingers, allowing me to weave easily. It was much finer than yarn. Grandma used the leftover hair strands to fashion dolls for me, and I named every doll Katie after the mother I never knew.

Distracted from my chores and with no sense of time, I got lost in play. Of course, there were no clocks in the funeral parlor. But there was a large tub tucked in the corner waiting to be filled with ice and slid under the coffin stretcher during the next funeral to keep decomposition at bay. When no one was looking, I submerged my Katie dolls in the tub and pretended to have them swim or drown.

Finally, I got around to my flower duty and found a handful of dried flowers: red carnations and baby's breath already days old and selected by Mrs. Jeffries for frugal reasons. These faded bunches of withered flowers, which had fallen from the final farewell of Mr. Jeffries's casket, were my property now. His funeral had been a rushed and cheap affair, which, to my way of thinking, was more than he deserved. Mr. Jeffries had been the worst kind of mean: He was friendly on the surface. Donning a good humor face, which he wore for the town, was a thin disguise. The whole town knew he was vile to his flesh and blood for no good reason.

I stuffed the dried-out flowers in the pocket of my dress. It was a cotton dress with an oversized square collar trimmed in a cheerful blue. A catalog dress, it was a splurge, and Grandma Wade made a big-to-do when it arrived. But it wasn't perfect until Grandma added a hidden pocket in the folds on the right side of the skirt. Due to its expense, this dress was expected to last me a long time. I felt it already tight in the bodice, but I didn't dare say a word; I'd just have to breathe less. Besides, the pocket housed tiny treasures found after funerals. Mourners were not observant and often dropped odds and ends as they shuffled about the parlor. These funerary leftovers were my delight.

As I headed up the stairs to my bedroom on the second floor, I was followed by Samael who was licking his lips. I was glad Samael had eaten Mr. Jeffries' soul. But I wondered if it didn't taste bad. I imagined the feast Samael had and smiled as I crushed the found flowers with the mortar and pestle, I'd taken from the kitchen. My grinding quickly pulverized the carnations and baby's breath into a coarse powder, which I poured back into my pocket.

Samael soundlessly followed me out to the now-vacant graveyard. He leaned against a mighty granite tombstone marked Katherine Wade, my mother, and picked his teeth with one of Mr. Jeffries's pinky finger bones.

He wasn't a big talker. I made enough noise for both of us, so it was no matter. I sang the tinny tune of Samael's favorite song, "After You've Gone." He would tell me later, when in one of his mean moods, that I sang off-key. I thought I sang in a young child's voice that some find sweet, like a heavenly choir, but I guess Samael liked my song because it chilled to the bone.

There'll come a time, now don't forget it.
There'll come a time when you'll regret it.
But baby, think what you're doin'.
I'm gonna haunt you so,
I'm gonna taunt you so,

It's gonna drive you to ruin.
After you've gone, after you've gone away.

I warbled with the confidence of the tone-deaf while I scattered the desiccated flower mixture over the graves like feeding scratch to chickens. My father wouldn't allow chickens. He said we didn't have the time. So, I pretended to have chickens. If anyone in the family had bothered to pay attention to me, they would have seen a convincing show of things. But the family did not mark my playful antics. It was only Death who engaged me.

An Angel of Death, Samael, had always been a part of my play. It took some time before I gave up on my family seeing Samael the way I could. And I learned Samael was just for me. As I tossed the powdery mixture about the graves, I was pretending to be a death-worn Cinderella toiling away and waiting for her prince charming. He looked a lot like Samael.

Chapter 3

How the Cookie Crumbles

2021

Anna

Anger flushed my cheeks as I slouched on the stool at the kitchen counter in our old house. I pouted as Mom explained that I did not need lipstick. I was too young.

"Anna, come taste this," Mom said, trying to move past the argument, but I dug in my heels. My thoughts ran in circles, looking for a new angle. But all my arguments were spent. I was at a dead end. What could I do?

I'll never speak again. That's what I'll do. That will teach her. She'll never hear my voice again. I'll be mute.

Abby busted into the house shouting at the top of her lungs, "Mom, Mom! I'm selling Girl Scout Cookies!" She still had her snow boots on and tracked the melting ice chunks from the front door, down the hall, and into the kitchen.

"Abby, that's great! Let me see," Mom said.

"Will you buy some?" Abby asked.

"Of course, we will. What do we have here?"

Oh, sure, we need cookies, but not lipstick.

"Get the Do-Si-Dos. I love that name," Abby giggled.

"Okay, let's see. Oh, the Samoas are my favorite. And Dad likes Shortbread."

"I want the Tagalongs," I said.

Damn! There goes my talking strike.

"And Thin Mints," I added sheepishly.

"Oh, the Thin Mints. I love those, too," Mom said, giving me a conspiratorial wink.

"I want them all," Abby said as she kicked off her boots and reached up to tighten her long blonde pony-tail.

"Okay, let's get a box of each and five boxes of Thin Mints," Mom said while she marked the form.

"Do you think Daddy could take it to work?" Abby said. "I hear that's a great way to sell cookies. And I want to win 'Most Sales' so I can get the Nintendo Switch."

"I agree. Because I don't think it is safe to go door to door and cross the street these days," Mom said.

"Oh, I'm so hungry. I wish we had these cookies right now!" Abby said.

She swung her hot pink stocking feet while perched on the kitchen stool. Her fingers were red and sticky from the remainder of a lollipop. The little white stick stuck out the side of her mouth and wobbled when she spoke, like the habit of a lifelong smoker. Abby had recently become enamored with spaghetti westerns. The tight-lipped smoker look was her latest trend.

"Me, too," I caved further to the bubble of excitement that had burst my resentment from a few moments before. "Can we make cookies?"

"Well, I've got the Nestle Tollhouse ready-to-bake. If you want?"

"Yeet," Abby and I rang out in unison.

***

And that's how the chocolate smear got on Georgie's left ear. Instead of cleaning him properly, Abby had sucked the chocolate from his ear. Now, Mom can't bring herself to wash the bear; nor do I want her to. The faint smudge of chocolate can still be seen even here as Georgie lay on the dusty linoleum floor of my new bedroom. Like a stalwart yet pudgy guardian, Georgie waits for my return. Leaving my new room, I walk to the doorway of the unfinished room. Already, I can tell the upstairs will be too much space for just me and Georgie.

The world seems too big and empty ever since Abby died. But I don't linger for long in this unwelcome space. Staying too long in the same spot, dwelling too long on Abby, always brings back the sorrow in crashing waves. I am overcome with the sensation of drowning. My chest grows tight, and my breathing becomes shallow and rapid. I have to keep moving and stay distracted to outpace this oppression. So, I leave Georgie and run downstairs to fetch Enoch, our pet cat, from his carrier. Enoch is a fat, long-haired ginger tabby. He is so fluffy. Abby and I used to bury our faces in his fur. Enoch tolerated our invasive affection. And he is my best friend when he cares to be, as this is the way with cats.

I capture and hog Enoch's affections every chance I get. And now, Enoch is the best defense against mice in this place. When I let Enoch loose in the house, the tension in my body begs off a bit. Begrudgingly, a grin spreads across my face as I watch him lumber away to explore.

All that first night, I toss and turn, tugging on my blanket, but something else, or someone else, seems to be pulling on it, too. The tug-of-war slumber keeps me from sleeping well and being warm. Curled in a fetal position, I shiver until I eventually fall asleep and dream of Abby. In my dream, I'm driving the car, and I can't stop it because I can't reach the pedals. The car refuses to stop no matter how much I scream or kick my legs. It just continues to barrel forward. Abby stands silently in the road in her Brownie uniform, staring right at me. The moment before impact, Abby screams, "Help Me!"

And then I wake up. This is what I call sleep every night since Abby died. But this time, waking up on a bare mattress on the second floor of a strange house is more than off-putting, and my enthusiasm from the day before seems childish.

How could I have thought this would be a good place?

Isolated upstairs, I miss our old ranch-style house with a pink bedroom for Abby and my purple bedroom. I miss my friends. I have even begun to miss our pain-in-the-ass neighbor Ian Harold. Ian was almost a year older than me, and he had teased me mercilessly about my slow ascent into puberty. I remember his insults with a flush to my cheeks and a tear in my eye, knowing the abuse would come no more.

***

"Hey, Anna Banana, I heard you were having a bad day," Ian said.

I walked to the mailbox while Abby played with Georgie and her Barbies in the front yard. Ian turned to his friend Corey.

"Anna knew she would have a bad day when she put her bra on backward, and it fit better," Ian hollered.

The boys roared with laughter. Ian lifted the hem of his red popsicle-stained t-shirt to wipe the drool from his chin.

***

I hated Ian, but now, here in this vacant house with only a smattering of my belongings, I miss Ian's drool, insults, and all. Even more so when Mom enters the room and starts going down the list of things to do today. I have charge of unboxing my stuff and keeping an eye on Enoch.

"Why do we have to live here?" I whine, refusing to roll over and face Mom.

"This is our chance for a new start," Mom explains for the seventeenth time through gritted teeth.

"Nobody cares about what I want," I holler over my shoulder as Mom storms from the room.

Reluctantly, I start to unpack. I empty a box of clothes on the bare mattress. A training bra flings out and lands on Georgie's remnant of a nose. The bear is in the line of fire, and he winds up strewn with a pile of socks and panties. But I don't care about Georgie at the moment. I don't want to be in this stupid, crumbling house.

When we arrived yesterday, I was not the only one deflated and instantly depressed at the appearance of the two-story fright. Initially, I tried not to let Mom and Dad know, but my feigned enthusiasm in selecting my new bedroom wanes in today's stale morning light. As I continue to haul more of my belongings from the U-Haul trailer, my desire to detach from and abandon the new family home comes out in bursts of anger. I bang my boxes into every porch post, door, and wall on the way to my new room.

I can't face the growing number of boxes in the ugly room. So, I leave the unpacked boxes to check and see if Enoch is adjusting to his litter box in this strange basement. It is a unique spot. It feels empty and crowded at the same time. And like all basements, despite the best efforts, it never feels homey. But this basement is a threatening hole in the ground. And no one is going to tell me differently. I clutch the railing and descend heavily down the wooden steps in my faux leather combat boots. I had been hasty with the litter box set-up the day before and only gave Enoch a smidgen of pellets. I'd dumped the litter box at the bottom of the stairs and galloped back to the first floor. I realize there isn't enough litter. There is shit on the floor.

I look around for the cat litter bag and simultaneously mark my surroundings. The basement is barren, dark, dank, and nearly all consumed in shadow. A bare bulb and string hang overhead, hovering with a halo of light above the washing machine and dryer, waiting for hook-up. Stark light illuminates more and less than I want to see. Once again, I flee the basement, task undone.

Forget the litter and the shit.

Wrinkling my nose, I leave the basement door cracked open so Enoch can come and go.

The entire time I'm unpacking, a dull ache grows in my gut. It does not go well with the mildew smell of the room, especially as this mustiness is accompanied by more than a hint of stale cigarettes.

God, this place is gross.

I detect a slight scratching noise. Meanwhile, my parents are preoccupied with getting the appliances hooked up and moving the larger pieces of furniture into the house. So, they cannot be bothered to tackle my problems, including getting Wi-Fi. All of my technology: my phone and the family computer, are dead. I have no connection to the outside world. I begin to think blocking out the world was an intentional act of cowardice on my parents' part. They are running away from life, away from the painful memories of Abby. I am also eager to escape the pain, but being young, I naturally want to live all the promises of life. Abby's absence does not mean an end to my dreams and desires.

As I sit on the floor in a ring of boxes, I am overwhelmed and underwhelmed at the same time. Nearly immobilized with anger and heartbreak, I manage the daunting task of unpacking. Again, the scratching noise comes, but this time it sounds closer. Since Enoch is off hunting somewhere else in the house, I go outside to find a mouse poking stick to clear the room, just in case. My poking and jabbing in corners comes clear, if not exactly clean. Then Mom enters with clean sheets, a candle, and my purple comforter.

"Here, make your bed."

"Me?"

"You. I'll be back with matches to light the candle to help clear some of that bad odor out of here. But you must be careful with a lit candle," Mom says.

Grief does nothing to counteract Mom's bossiness.

Earlier, Mom and Dad had put the frame of my bed together; now, I need to figure out which corner of the fitted sheet to start with. I never get that right. I make the bed, but only because I don't want to look at the bare striped mattress anymore. It screams homelessness; a glaring reminder of my life being stripped down. After wrestling with the fitted sheet, I slowly unpack more boxes.

Why do I have so much shit?

I immediately regret unpacking; I don't want to make this place home. I hate this space without Abby.

After a nap from depression and boredom, I wake to find the sun deep in setting. I hear the call for dinner; what was a holler down the hall at home is now a muffled crow from the first floor here. As usual, with naps, I wake up in a worse mood. I don't want to be here. In my dream, I'd been hunting for a bathroom, but I couldn't find one and couldn't control myself. I touch a wet spot on the sheets.

Jesus, did I pee the bed?

But this isn't urine. It is red. I finally start my period in the middle of a creepy desolate house with no friends to tell. I bury my face in Georgie and bellow. For a moment, I think I might cry real tears, but actual tears are hard to come by these days. I have cried myself out about Abby's passing. Yet the pain still festers inside, and there are no more tears to let go.

I yearn for yesterday, and I don't know how to live in a world without Abby. I am coming to find I don't even know who I am without Abby. My identity disintegrated in the freezing rain that February night. All my memories of Abby are already tired and worn, faded and soft, and not enough. These memories are silent and staid like Georgie. The color and joy seeps from them. And just like Georgie, no matter how huggable a toy can be, it cannot return love; it can only receive. The memories are like a drain, like a sieve, a little more washing away with each recall. Georgie received all the love and affection Abby had to give him. I try my best to absorb Abby's love back out of Georgie. But this is not the natural course for teddy bears. While I attempt to annex Abby's love, I drown Georgie in little muffled screams. My suppressed angst rankles with another call for dinner.

I thump my way down the stairs and through the kitchen to sit at the head of the dining room table in the sunroom. Purposefully sitting in Mom's spot, but Mom and Dad don't bite the bait, and they sit on either side of me.

"What am I supposed to do out here?" I ask as I dish out three healthy heaps of Stovetop dressing.

"Give it time. We all need to heal," Dad says, placing a pork chop on my plate.

"That's easy for you to say. You leave on a trip tomorrow for your new job, and we're stuck here. And I don't want this," I say, forking the pork chop aggressively and putting it on his plate.

"Be patient," Mom says, although I know she feels the same way. "And you need to eat something more than carbs."

"I'm a vegetorion," I say, shoving a forkful of stuffing into my mouth.

"It's vegetarian, and since when?" Mom challenges.

"Since this pork chop. It's overcooked and sad."

We eat in silence without even the clink of cutlery on china. No one has unpacked the plates and utensils yet. Mom had dug out paper plates and plastic utensils from the picnic basket on the kitchen counter. It was easier to identify the picnic basket than hunt through many boxes. Mom chooses the easy way every time since Abby's death. She doesn't have the steam to do more. She doesn't have the energy to be a wife and mother. The soft plastic slide on paper probably sounds defeat to my wilting Mom. It sounds like a triumph to me, the vegetarian.

I am open to talking when Mom comes by my room for lights out. I sit again on a bare mattress with a library book we had forgotten to return back in St. Louis. The wadded-up sheets are on the floor.

"What happened? I thought you made this bed," Mom says.

"I started my period. I need a new sheet."

"What? When? Why didn't you tell me?"

"You were so busy with the move; I didn't want to be a bother," I mumble.

"Anna, I'm sorry. You can always come to me. I will

always be here for you."

"Well, I'm telling you now. Besides, I knew what to do. I just didn't know where to find a clean sheet."

"Okay, but I'm so proud of you. You are becoming a woman. You know, I noticed you were starting to look a little curvy. This is so exciting," Mom says.

"Mom, gross," I say, wrinkling up my nose to hide my embarrassment. "And actually, it's crampy."

"I'll get something for that, too."

She kisses the top of my head and hurries away with the stained sheet.

"Jesus, she's acting like it's some kind of party," I say to the empty room, which I have to admit doesn't feel so empty at the moment. When Mom returns to help make the bed, it is the closest to feeling tucked-in that I have experienced in years. It just seemed babyish before. Now, it is consoling, and from the look in her eyes, Mom finds it a comfort, too. I wonder why I had shut down our bedtime routine a few years ago and contemplate if it is too late to get it back.

Pulling the purple comforter tight, I shrink inside the darkness that seems to stretch from the origins of the furthest corner, seeping out from under the closet door. The closet is shut. Everyone knows that all closets have to be closed when going to bed.

A black shadow of substance cracks open the closet door, sliding it aside just a little. The shadow slithers out and across the room, enveloping and cradling me. It is thick and just this side of suffocating. I tell myself it is my imagination. Soon, I am fast asleep.

Chapter 4

A Family History

1918

Beverly

I WAS BORN IN 1911, and I was the only child my parents had who would live beyond a year old. None of my siblings lived beyond the bassinet in my parents' bedroom. So, the nursery on the backside of the second floor, which received the morning light, was left unfinished. The walls had been studded out, and the floor was laid in gray linoleum. But there were no furnishings. It was a lonely space.

Two windows were fitted looking out into the backyard and the cemetery behind the carriage house, which was turned into a garage with the popularity of cars. Only a tall adult could see much from these windows. The cemetery was a peek-a-boo from this view. The outlines of three prayerful stone angels marked the resting places of my siblings.

With the passing of each baby, my family came to consider themselves cursed, as if doing death's work had made the Wade family unworthy of welcoming life.

With the death of each baby, hope eroded.

As my grandma would tell it, I was born in the Wade House, like my deceased siblings, in the upper bedroom that had once been an empty attic space. My parents' bedroom at the time was a bare spot surrounded by unfinished construction. My mother experienced hard labor for two days with me. Each time her cries of pain eased and faded, they left behind an ominous silence.

My grandma wiped her daughter-in-law's face and encouraged her with soft words. "Oh, God, please," she said while applying a fresh towel to my mother's brow. My grandma was afraid to ask for too much, for a healthy baby and a healthy new mother. Her mouth was full of wishes, but she was scared silent. Suddenly, strength returned to my overwrought mother, and I was born in six desperate pushes.

Grandma and the midwife happily counted ten fingers and ten toes. At the same time, Death took advantage of the situation and escorted my spent mother away. From that day forward, Samael and my family had a cold relationship. The family begrudged what they saw as Death's greed. He had taken the previous three Wade babies. Would his hunger for souls ever be satisfied? Samael was indifferent to the incident. His purpose was to take all and any souls on the cusp of life.

After much argument, my father and grandfather planted a peach tree to the left of the house. A place near enough and far enough to satisfy neither of them. My father wanted the peach tree close to the home because it was an old way of warding off evil. But given the family business, Grandpa worried the tree would also ward off death.

Father pleaded, "The tree cannot ward off death. It can only guard against evil. Death is neither evil nor good in its natural state. Death is just a part of life. But

Death has become so comfortable here it heeds not its purpose. Death eats and eats. I do not wish to put an end to the family business, a necessity of life. I just wish to guard my child against premature death. The tree is a deterrence for gluttony and evil."

He stopped talking when he heard his logic, which was convoluted and rooted in silly superstition. Still, he backed his argument with earnest designs to protect me, his only daughter. His shirt was untucked, and he fidgeted like a child in front of his father and raised a hand to his worried brow; he sighed in his closing argument. He simply wanted to protect me.

The argument was legendary, and Grandma used to tell it to me as a bedtime story. She thought it was a story of protection and love. It filled me with fear and distrust of my grandfather.

Grandpa Wade eventually agreed to the tree, but he had ideas about securing his business against any interference from this peach tree. Samael liked to linger at the back of the kitchen where the men argued. He found their discourse amusing.

"Like a peach tree can ward off death or evil," he would chuckle.

He left the men to their superstitions and recessed upstairs in the shadows of my closet.

My second-floor room, with the setting sun's light, had been a place to tuck me away, a space to keep "the child" without strings to attach the family to another baby they thought would pass. The sun faded away each day, and unexpectedly I grew more robust, and so did the peach tree. I lived, and the tree soared.

As a small child, I stared outside the single dormer window of my room, viewing all the colors of the sunset across this small opening onto the sky. The light that filtered through the window was a rosy, then a bluing hue, creating a soft and comforting mood. I climbed my large brass bed where I and all my dead siblings had been born. Clinging to the posts and balancing my bare feet on the pipes beneath me, I strained to see more of the colorful nature show. In the twilight, I faced this solitary window and marked the close of day. Then the festival of stars would shine for me as I sat atop a worn quilt of multi-colored concentric rings and a thin white sheet covering the blood-stained mattress that recorded all the messy details of the ill-fated births and my mother's death.

Reading *Alice in Wonderland* for the umpteenth time, I was waiting for Samael when I heard him slip into my room and settle into the darkest corner. Although I had the luxury of my own bedroom and indoor plumbing, when many children in town still slept several to a bed and had outhouses, I felt my life wrecked by a kind of scarcity. To my way of thinking, I had it all and nothing at the same time.

"Where have you been? I was reading and waiting for you," I said.

"*Alice in Wonderland*, again?"

"Of course, not that there is much to choose from the collection of books about the Dead," I said.

Samael sounded tired. But still, I wanted to play.

"Let's play, Samael."

I tucked my chin and looked up at him. Samael did not answer. I thought I looked coy and wondered if he saw my intention. Samael was not familiar with flirting—neither was I. I was basing my looks on silent film stars Lillian Gish and Clara Bow from the Saturday Matinee in town.

Samael understood looks of fear, desperation, and anger, sure. But flirting didn't come up in his line of work. Observing my young girl's clumsy attempts at flirtation was perplexing for him.

I gave forth an overblown pout that I was pretty sure made me look like I was about to be sick. I could tell by the way he withdrew ever so slightly with a flare to his nostrils and a crease to his brow. I was not pulling this off. I wanted to look like the silver screen beauty I'd seen in the moving pictures last week. We had the same doe eyes and loose curls, but where she was a damsel in distress, I think I came off as a demented child.

I blinked long and slow and wished I had title cards to get my point across. Although to be honest, I wasn't sure what I was aiming for. But this was real life, not the movies, and I was frustrated. I blew out the breath I had been holding but not realizing I was holding, and it made a raspberry sound that put an end to my femme fatale fiasco. I returned to the blunt edge of innocence.

"Can I have some of your shimmery feathers?"

He sidled up close. "Of course."

He seemed relieved at the shift in discourse. That was until he gave me a slow, long blink and protruded his bottom lip with a slump to his shoulder. I shuddered. God, did I look that bad? When he tried to mimic my flirtation, he looked unnaturally hungry. It would not be Samael's or my last attempt or failure at flirting.

Samael unfurled his wings while crouching in the shadows. The wings were enormous on a young man of his size, and in the corner, they were cramped and could not fully extend. He shuddered, and a bunch of black and green-tinged feathers floated to the ground. I scuttled about collecting my boon.

"Oh, thank you!"

I was pleased enough to hug him, but no one hugs Death. I happily accepted the molted feathers and turned my focus to a game I understood: dolls. As Samael retired once more to a position of comfort, I got to crafting a feathered cradle for my dolls. Then I stitched the remaining feathers to the back of a teddy bear. The black angel feathers gleamed and caressed the teddy bear, and I positioned it next to the dolls in their cradle where he could watch over them. I wished I had a bed of black angel wings to rest in or, better yet, beautiful black wings of my own.

Chapter 5

What Goes Unsaid

2021

Anna

AN UNCOMFORTABLE SILENCE GROWS between Mom and me as we attempt to hang the wrong wallpaper in my room. The pink wallpaper has tiny white flowers, perfect for Abby. Once again, I feel like the wrong daughter has died. Despite all this, I act almost chatty amid the furniture draped in old white sheets and moving blankets. I sit among the gummy brushes, rags, and bucket of glumpy glue, trying to think of something to say. Between the dingy ghost-like protrusions of my bed and the chifforobe, I bubble with babble.

Most of my furniture sits in the living room downstairs, awaiting Dad's return. He'd conveniently gone away on a business trip to Cincinnati with his new job. Doing what? I have no idea, but work always seemed more important than myself, Mom, and even Abby.

Dad had tried to hide his enthusiasm to bail on us. But the hurry with which he left belied his apologies and promises to make things up to us when he returned. Since Mom and I cannot move the desk and mirrored dresser up the narrow staircase, Mom decides to move on to cleaning and decorating.

Cleaning has minimal impact as most of the stains are stubborn. The dust and dirt have gotten used to having full reign in this house. Try as Mom might, the house will not give over so easily to her scrubbing and scouring. I observe Mom in what appears to be a futile race to nowhere, and I just try to stay out of her way. I don't want to be enlisted in the unproductive onslaught of housewifery.

If Mom can't beat the time-stamped soiled spots out, she will cover them. While we struggle to perk up my bedroom with new wallpaper, I succumb to the sudden temptation to talk to Mom like a girlfriend. I would have died for a girlfriend to talk to out here on the edge of nowhere, especially since I have just started my period. But all I have is a scowling mother with a lump of glue in her hair. The attempt to get chatty briskly proves to be a pointless effort. Without a best friend to confide in, the "official, stamp-of-approval" transition into puberty has gone from something I had long hoped for, a milestone of adolescence, into a bloody inconvenience. Instead of girly giggles, this hallmark of womanhood doubles me down with cramps, and the heavy flow pad fits like a diaper. The whole experience is a letdown.

Mom struggles with another mismeasured sheet of wallpaper sliding off the wall. Together we try to hold the strip of wallpaper in place. Mom stretches to reach the top of the gluey sheet, while I stand just under her, holding my section in place. The sour whiff of coffee on Mom's breath taints the air and filters over my face. I try breathing into my sleeve to avoid the stink. Our arms burn from the strain, forcing us to release our hold.

Within seconds, the sheet of glumpy wallpaper surrenders to the floor.

The fumes aren't helping; both of us have booming headaches. We have papered three-quarters of the room when each 2-foot by 8-foot strip slinks off the walls, dropping in rumpled plops on the floor. Mom looks even more defeated than before. And I understand precisely how she feels. But I refuse to give Mom any support. In lieu of a punching bag, I am taking my anger out on the only other person in the house.

"Dad would have hung it right."

Mom says nothing.

I wonder if she agrees or is too tired of my barbed comments.

Feeling remorse, I remark, "I don't want wallpaper anyway."

To my dismay, this comment does nothing to remove the sting of the previous statement.

"Let's go have lunch," Mom says and walks out the door. A scrap of wallpaper sticks to the bottom of her New Balance tennis shoe.

Now, I am discouraged. Apparently, I am a failure of a daughter. I had wanted to engage Mom in an argument, but she is overcome by the weight of this dump in the wake of Abby's passing. I look about the room. It looks like a giant paper-mâché project gone awry. Our efforts to brighten this space have made the room look darker and more depressing. The moldy walls, greased over with sticky goo, give off the Hollywood effect of slime running down the walls—like in *Ghostbusters*. Abby and our parents loved that movie. Dad declared it a classic when he selected it for family movie night. I, primarily out of belligerence, found the film outdated. And I still wonder which Ghostbuster was supposed to be the cute one.

The cheery bits of wallpaper that are sticking just amplify the sense of decay in the room's dark corners. I shake my head in disappointment over the room and myself, then I go to wash the sticky, itchy goop off my hands before going downstairs to have lunch with Mom. As I wash my hands under the small stream of warm water, the goop sticks to the porcelain sink and clogs the drain. I use a towel to clean the basin, which ruins the towel, but does little to relieve the clog in the drain. I decide I will just have to use hand sanitizer in this bathroom until Dad returns. Waiting for Dad is the best choice over telling Mom that I have clogged the drain. I simply can't face being any more of a disappointment to her.

The toxic odor from the failed wallpapering lingers like the clay from a wet grave clings to a shoe. And I know that smell well since I followed Mom, rain or shine, to Abby's grave every day for the first month. After that, I couldn't go anymore. It was too depressing, and besides, Mom stopped inviting me. As the windows in my room had been painted shut years earlier, fresh air is impossible, and the fumes choke me ruthlessly.

The poor ventilation must have aggravated our bad dispositions. Down in the sunroom, the natural light does little to lift my mood, and Mom slinks even further down a slippery slope into a grim slump.

"I'm sorry," I mumble to the plate of peanut butter and jelly sandwich with a side of Pringles. I flex my fingers, pitting and clawing at the soft wood of the table in my nervous state. Digging small crescent-shaped marks into the over-waxed table. Detritus of wood polish and grime scrape off the table and embed under my nails.

"No, you're right. I wish your father were here, too," Mom says.

I want to tag Abby onto that sentiment, but we are

both feeling this so keenly it needn't be said.

"Your Dad should be home next week as long as this business trip doesn't get extended," Mom says. "It's just bad timing with the moving-in and all."

I understand Mom is right, but this doesn't ease my sense of abandonment or growing frustration. Shunted aside since Abby's death, even my hugs and cuddles are a mere pacifier for my parents' grief. My affections are not about me. They are about Abby. Everything belongs to Abby, which is precisely why they moved us here—in an attempt to erase Abby and all the pain that came with remembering.

My agitation makes me long for control. I acutely want to make something happen and take force over some aspect of my life. Right now, and for a while, my life has been shit.

As if Mom can read my mind, she says, "Don't forget to check on the cat litter. And be careful on those basement stairs."

This is not the kind of control I hoped for. Tossed about on the seas of fate, I lose my appetite and gaze out one of the many windows in the sunroom. I stare into the vacant yard. Then I see a dark figure at the edge of the yard. The sun creates a glare on the window, making the figure appear blurred. But then he comes into focus.

I am surprised to see anyone in the lot, not to mention a teenage boy. I want to go out and introduce myself, but I am chicken shit. I wipe my face and count three pimples on the bridge of my nose and one on my chin.

Jesus! Why did I slack on my face wash?

Then I tighten my long dark blonde ponytail, and I weigh my scrubby looks against my desire.

YOLO

Meanwhile, Mom drones on about unpacking

Abby's boxes tucked inside the small, dark room just off her bedroom. Now, I am even more compelled to go outside. I want to know about this boy who is oddly dressed in a white, long-sleeved button-down shirt and dark slacks in this heat.

Why is he here of all places?

Where did he come from?

He stands poised with a dark blazer draped over one arm, and the other hand shoved in his pants pocket. He looks ready, like he is waiting for me. His appearance suggests one of recently coming from church or a funeral. It is a Tuesday afternoon, so it couldn't be a wedding.

I review my glue-smeared t-shirt and glue-crusted jeans. I want to clean up but don't want to miss him. He turns toward the back of the property with the overgrown area behind the dilapidated garage, which is in such poor shape we can't even park the car there.

"I'm going to go outside for some air," I announce and abruptly scoot back from the table.

I can't take any more of Mom's grief, and I do indeed need some fresh air. As I turn the glass doorknob and look over my shoulder, I pause, uncertain if Mom is deeply contemplating her bologna sandwich or dwelling over the family's loss. Either way, what she is really doing is ignoring me. Something she never did before Abby's Death.

The screen door slams shut behind me, alerting the boy, who turns around and watches as I cross the yard. He doesn't smile, but something about his presence is welcoming. I walk toward him, looking for snakes in the tall grass. There is something odd about the land here, but I can't put my finger on it. The steps I make in the dead vegetation should make some muffled crunch, but they don't. Then I realize the oddity of the yard lays buried in the silence: no birds, no insects, no life of any kind. Everything is dead.

The still silence runs deep as if this place fell into a profound slumber long ago, like Sleeping Beauty. There is the sense that I have disturbed something unmarked. Something I very much want to stay dead, and it crawls upon my skin and sends shivers down my back. More than this case of the willies, I can't take the silence, the nothing. Most of all, I try to shirk the void in my head that leaves a metallic taste in my mouth. Then I crack the unnatural quiet with my introduction.

"Hi, I'm Anna." My voice sounds loud and broken.

When did that happen?

"I'm Sam. Nice to meet you," he says. He is wearing dark brown pleated trousers and dress shoes. The kind of shoes that should be shined, but his are not. They have scuff marks like he'd been laboring in them doing dirty, physical work.

"Do you live around here? I kinda thought we were all alone," I say.

"Oh, I've been here a long time," he says, tapping his forefinger against his thumb like he wants to pinch something.

"Do you live nearby?" I ask.

"Yes."

He bares a grin of overcrowded teeth, a bit like Freddie Mercury. Reflexively, I roll my tongue along my braces. I wanted Invisalign, but my parents said that was a luxury for responsible types, which pissed me off, and this is precisely why. I'm standing in front of the most attractive real-life boy I've ever seen with a caged smile.

I glance around, but there is nothing nearby. Just empty lots that repeat over and over an exaggeration of the depleted, dried-up fields of prairie grass in a drought. I decide it would be rude to press him further on his origins.

"So, what are you doing over here?"

"I like to visit the cemetery. It is quiet, and I think the dead need company. You know?"

"Um, what? A cemetery?"

"Behind your garage. That overgrown area with the desiccated Aster, Ashy Sunflowers, and purple-headed sneezeweed," Sam says.

I guffaw, and a little spit escapes my mouth. I think the spittle lands on his cheek, but he doesn't flinch or move to wipe anything from his face.

Well, spitting on the guy is one surefire way to draw attention to my mouth grill, which is probably glinting in the afternoon sun.

"Purple-headed sneezeweed? That's hilarious."

I abruptly suck up my mirth as he isn't laughing. I, of all people, should know there is nothing funny about a cemetery.

"Do you want to see?" he says.

I am tired of death, but I am just getting a taste for teenage boys, so I say, "Yes."

Together we walk through the tall grass and weeds, which wilt even more in our passing. We arrive at the cemetery's edge, and I can see the tops of tombstones dotting the narrow but long plot of land inside. A tremendous black wrought iron fence and gate keep us out of the graveyard.

Is it here to keep people out or the dead in?

Some graves look more freshly dug or disturbed than others. This is weird. Here the silence echoes an emptiness growing in the pit of my stomach like a hole opening, flowering deep inside me. The sensation swells and sticks in my diaphragm. It makes it hard to breathe.

"Who are these people?" I say in a whisper, scrunching my toes inside my shoes.

"They once lived here in the town, but they have been forgotten over time," Sam says.

"That's awful."

I think about Abby and how far we moved from her grave.

Who will remember Abby? Visit her grave?

Suddenly, my guilt over Abby grows more substantial, along with my grief.

Sam smiles at me again. I squat and start pulling the dry overgrowth away from the nearest stone. I want something to do besides looking grief-stricken. The quick crumble of dirt dusts my sweaty palms, and the crunch of dead vegetation disintegrates in my hands. I read the worn inscription, Caroline Dawson 1899–1922.

I do the math in my head. "That's a long time ago. But she was not that old."

"Death does not discriminate," Sam says.

"I know," I say.

My knees sink into the soft earth.

Shouldn't the ground here be firm?

On my knees, I take a closer look at Sam's shoes. The creased and shabby brown leather brogues are dusted with chunks of dirt.

Has he been digging in the graveyard?

I keep my head bowed, trying to hide my guilt and curiosity, making myself busy by picking at the crust of glue on my jeans. Then I rally to make the most of this moment alone with a boy. I stand up and dust the crush of dried dirt from my pants.

"You know?" Sam asks.

"My little sister died six months ago." Adding hurriedly, "It was an accident."

I hope the words will make it feel like a genuine accident, but instead, they bloat in my mouth, gagging with the burden of fault.

I turn to Sam. He has a knowing look like he has experienced loss. But he seems comfortable with death, whereas I wrestle with death.

My anxiety flourishes. I want to stay out here with this mysterious boy. His dark eyes penetrating my very being, elevating me to something real, alive, more than the shadow of Abby that I have become in my own family. His intensity instills a desire to know him better. Yet, he wears a darkness about him that makes me wary and reminds me of stranger danger, so I say goodbye and hope to see him again. Sam says he is sure of it and watches as I walk back to the house.

A dragonfly whirs above my head as I approach the back steps. I brush at the insect with my hand, suddenly keenly noticing the sound it makes, which crests with the soft chirp of birds nesting in the eaves of the garage. The peep of small life lurks on the edge of this desolate place. The sounds snag on my attention, ripping me free of the gossamer shroud of yearning thoughts of Sam. I turn to wave at him, but he is already gone.

Chapter 6

Wade or Wicked?

1921

Beverly

THIS WAS NEVER GOING to work. But I was determined to try.

I stood on the wobbly, wooden kitchen stool, which I had dragged inside the bathroom, so I could get a good look at myself in the mirror. Like every generation of the Wade family, I had thick blonde hair and a cowlick on the top of my head. This cowlick caused me to spend many hours in front of the mirror. Nothing had tamed it—until now, hopefully. I balanced the tub of lard on the back of the commode, scooped out a greasy portion with three fingers, and slicked it across my head. The cowlick was subdued.

"Yes!" I declared victory to my reflection in the mirror and smiled.

However, this new look was obvious, so I grabbed my father's comb from the sink and combed more lard through my hair from the roots to the ends, suffocating the curls into submission.

"I hope Samael will like it," I whispered to myself with a look of pride.

I stood for a while admiring my work. Then I heard Grandma enter the kitchen; I wondered how to replace the lard without getting caught. I listened carefully to the tap of Grandma's hard-soled shoes on the tiled kitchen floor until I heard her exit the back door which clunked when it swung shut. I jumped off the rickety stool and made my way to the kitchen to return the tub of lard.

Next, I roamed all the shadowy places looking for Samael to show off my new hairdo, failing to realize the new lard-laden hairdo would give my theft away.

As I grew older, I would become adept at wearing my hair in a swept-up fashion, pinning down any rogue curls. But even with the efforts to hide the Wade cowlick, I could do nothing to warm the Wade's deep-set chilly blue eyes. I smiled a lot, like a strawberry festival queen, to put a cheer on my cold face, but as I lived and worked in the family business of a death hospital, my happy efforts came off as creepy. People whispered, wondering why I had a forced smile. What did I know that they did not? I was doomed to a lonely existence, except for Samael.

Even as a child, I understood that, on the business side, the Wade Death Hospital and Funeral Home were necessary to meet the needs of the St. Germaine community in lean times and in times of abundance. My family discovered early on a penchant for unidentified corpses, and it became a niche of the Wade Death Hospital and Funeral Home. Counties far and wide would have John Doe and Jane Doe bodies carted to our home. And, as they were all too glad to have the unidentified corpses off their hands, they'd pay a good price for the service.

All the bodies were delivered to the back of the house and taken in at the basement entrance. Here the adults in my family kept vigil until they confirmed more or less the person was indeed dead. The back entrance was accessed through cement steps dug ten feet deep under the house from the backyard. This would be a root cellar in most homes, but not here. A white-washed, wide-mouth double door fit at the bottom of these concrete stairs and was the entry for the men and corpses to move through comfortably.

A damaged corpse was bad for viewing and, thus, for business. But in the middle of the night, when heavy with sleep themselves, grandfather and father sometimes bumbled the bodies. It was all part of the behind-the-scenes action with unwrapped bodies and the stink of sick still wafting off the newly dead. This part of death was less than ceremonious and was built on practicalities.

The actual death chamber where bodies became prepared corpses ran underneath the width of the front of the house, directly under the funeral parlor. A concrete wall and two sets of thick, white-washed wooden doors sectioned off the death chamber from the rest of the basement. Twelve elevated concrete slabs spread out in two long rows inside this room.

This was plenty until we had trouble keeping up with the dead during the flu pandemic. In the otherwise empty basement, bodies filled the space, lined head to toe in various stages of rot. The cellar teemed with death, and my family worked around the clock shuffling bodies, quickly washing and dressing the dead. They laid them out in pre-constructed caskets.

It wasn't enough. We Wades had a tireless work ethic but developed a morally corrupt execution in this wave of death. My father and grandparents worked at night to hide their shortcuts. Digging up the dead for more caskets.

"Help me lift this one out," Grandfather Wade grunted as he gripped the ropes in his leather gloves. The rain was making everything slick.

"I got this end. Ready? One, Two, Three," called Father over the howl of the wind.

The casket slipped a little, and the rope wrapped tight around Father's left forearm slithered and dug into his flesh, leaving a rope burn. He gritted his teeth and hissed in pain. Together, my grandfather and father renewed their efforts and lifted the casket back to the surface, where it sank into the mud.

Opening the casket with a crowbar, they cracked open the top, then reached in and unceremoniously dragged the body out. Grandfather made a pointless wipe across his rain-soaked face. My father bent over, cradling his forearm in his stomach and taking deep breaths. His pants were stained with soil, his shirt soaked through, and a thin trace of his own blood left its mark upon his shirt.

"On the count of three?" Father called.

Grandfather gave a heavy nod. "I'll take the shoulders."

As they grasped and fumbled for a good hold on the shoulders and ankles of the dead woman, rain puddled in the corners of Mrs. Augustine's eyes like pools of tears reanimating her features under the strikes of lightning. And then her mouth popped open in a silent scream. The men, used to such things, jolted. And without a countdown, they dumped the body into the hole with the muffled flump of a bag of bones. There was no time to rest; the longer they took, the more they risked getting caught. They quickly filled in the hole.

This malpractice of burial was born under pressure

to bury more bodies than they had the manpower during the flu pandemic. But this practice also fructified our family. This casket removal and resale saved them time, labor, and money. Samael told me all of this with much delight later when he was tucked up in the dark corner of my closet.

With the corpse safely buried—again—Grandma cleaned away the muck and perfumed the casket for the next funeral.

"Amazing Grace, how sweet the sound that saved a wretch like me," Grandma sang sweetly as she worked, looking for leaky death stains on the satin lining of the recently vacated casket.

Her song trailed her movements from the clean casket over to the death chamber, where she gave a quick rinse of the next waiting corpse's face. All bodies with a viewing would be laid out in a suit or long-sleeved dress of black. So, Grandma Wade really only needed to clean the hands and face. If the body belonged to one of the more religious families, she didn't even need to touch up the ravages of time and sickness with a soft palette of makeup. The deeply devout and the unclaimed made for the easiest funerals and burials.

"I want to help," I piped up from a half-finished casket where I was hiding.

Grandma Wade didn't have the time to inquire as to whom I was hiding from today.

"Okay, get the makeup from the shelf," Grandma said.

"Can I paint her?" I asked.

"Well, I guess you have to learn sometime. I'll angle the light, and you start with that wax. Start light. I don't want to wash that ugly mug again."

"It's not ugly. It's sad," I argued. "The folds of fat and worry tell a sad story. I think."

The dead often seemed sad to me, and my family often felt selfish to me to prey upon the grieving and the grieved in the way they did. If my family had been insects, they'd have been like the locusts in the Bible.

I did not particularly like the turn of events that the flu pandemic had brought on. These changes were not exactly bad, but they were wrong, like not changing the sheets for a guest—even though we rarely had guests that were alive. I missed the sweet, clean scent of freshly hewn wood, which was fading in this new recycled approach to caskets. Those new caskets had been one of my favorite hiding places, but they were all gone or occupied now. I had just been hiding in one of the small, cracked caskets. It would be filled by the next child to die. I liked to think I was warming it up for the next occupant.

However, Grandfather Wade was vindicated. All this time, he had been feeding the peach tree with the drained blood of the dead. Or so reported a lip-smacking Samael one evening. Grandfather figured the blood would act like a sacrifice to the Angel of Death.

While Grandfather couldn't see Samael, he was a big believer. So, when the buckets of blood from the slabs were full, he took them out the wide-mouthed cellar doors, up the concrete steps, and poured them into a small pit near the left of the stairs. Blood soaked into the soil, and nothing ever grew there. One night, as he poured out the sticky slop, he got the idea to kill the peach tree. Business boomed, but pettiness ruled Grandfather Wade's heart. Under the dark of night, he poured three pails of blood into the soil at the base of the peach tree. The first two buckets went slow and steady. The ground made a sickening squelching glug as the roots drank deep, gulping down the blood offering. Then he dumped the remaining third bucket in one big slosh that sprayed back and stained his trousers. Samael swore the tree sighed with satisfaction. I know Samael did. Over time, the tree took on a dark gleam to its bark. No one knew what to make of this creepy tree except Grandfather and, secretly, me. Grandfather took over the task of dumping all the blood and every time fed it to the tree.

Over the years, the tree only produced rotten fruit, and Grandfather was pleased. He smiled that deep creased smile of the old and wicked.

Chapter 7
The Shrine

2021

Anna

I BACK INTO THE box of Lucky Charms, tipping it over and spilling cereal across the floor. Marshmallow tools of superstition skitter across the linoleum and gum onto my sock. The humidity in this attic space makes everything sticky—except the wallpaper.

I ignore the mounting mess of marshmallows, cereal, magazine scraps, and stinky wallpaper glue and focus on hanging the carefully snipped pictures of celebrities from my prized fashion magazine collection. I've had this particular pile of magazines for a few months now. I really miss getting them from the grocery store when we did the weekly shopping. Out here, Mom has groceries delivered by reluctant young adults who climb the porch with fear of a cave-in. One guy set the groceries on the cracked sidewalk and honked as he pulled away.

I don't know why Mom couldn't tag on a *Seventeen* or *Glitter* magazine to the online grocery order. With the promise from Mom of a new magazine soon, which is going the way of the promise of internet, I make a bold move to cut up these old fashion rags. I'm using the wallpaper glue to paste the pictures inside my closet after the Elmer's glue stick proved unable to do the job. I am having much more success than we ever had with the wallpaper.

I shake and flick my fingers to remove the excess glue and end up with small clumps of glue on the wall and on my clothes that I'd pushed to the back of the closet. Ignoring that, I smile at my handiwork.

I have fashioned a shrine to fashion. A Mecca to the images of celebrities ripped from the pages I have thumbed so many times. My shrine perfectly captures the hodgepodge of wishes and desires of my adolescent heart.

This particular issue of *Teen Vogue* had a lot of pictures, including Taylor Swift, Ariana Grande, and Zendaya. God, what I wouldn't give to look like any of these women. Instead, I have mousy blonde hair that always needs washing. It is eternally oily. I tried to get Mom to buy dry shampoo, anything to control this lanky mess of hair, but Mom couldn't fathom dry shampoo as a real thing. She says it's a gimmick, a product to prey upon my insecurities.

I had begged her, "Mom, please, can you order me some dry shampoo? I don't like using your shampoo. I don't like the minty green bathroom. And I swear that shower is out of a horror movie. It's really kind of creepy."

"It's not creepy," Mom lied. "It's just old with some rust stains. And I'll be able to clean that ring out of the tub when I find the right cleanser. As for the 'dry' shampoo, you don't need it. You have hair just like Abby. You don't want to change that."

"I'm not Abby," I said flatly. My begging had dried up.

"No. I know you're not. But you're still not getting the shampoo."

"Re-question. Cherry Coke?"

"What?" Mom looked into my face for clarity, but I only delivered an eye roll.

I added a brush of my oily hair sweeping over my shoulder. It was my best condescension, and I risked a reprimand with my sass. "Can you at least order soda this time? Cherry Coke?"

"Yeah, right, sure," Mom said, giving up the battle to later face the war.

"And is anyone going to do anything about the internet and the TV?" I continued to poke her with my disgruntled tone.

"I'm working on it. Do you think I enjoy hiking six miles to place an online grocery order or arguing with AT&T? Because I don't, and I don't like waiting through an automated phone system in the summer heat just to be disconnected. I'm done. I am done with that. Your Dad will deal with it when he returns."

"Yeah, when he returns with our only car. After he has stranded us out here," I said.

"Anna, we can't afford to fly right now, so he had to drive. Money is a little tight since I haven't returned to work. We have a second car on the list of things to do. On top of that, your dad saddled us with this wreck of a house that desperately needs to be updated to be livable. I mean, seriously, whoever heard of a house without even a functioning phone jack. Now, what do you want first? Because we can't have everything you want exactly when you want it. Please, be patient."

***

I use an ad for Clearasil to scoop up the cereal and dump it into the toilet adjacent to my bedroom. There is no way I am eating anything off this floor. I am not being wasteful. This is self-preservation.

I make a lazy effort to remove the excess glue from my fingers and cuticles, but cleaning up seems futile since I still need to finish the shrine and will have to wash the glue all off again. I decide to return to the business of creating and make do with the itchy, sticky mess on my hands.

Who should I paste up next?

I shuffle through the pictures on the floor with my big toe, the nail painted in purple polish that had gone on glumpy and chipped off. I desperately need a pedicure and a manicure. I promise myself to paint my nails as soon as I find my mani-pedi supplies.

I select a photo of Billie Eilish in a corset and realize I also have a photo of Bella Hadid in a corset and even Hailey Bieber in a corset. It's decided. I will save up my babysitting money to buy a corset for when my boobs finally come in.

But who can I babysit out here?

I think of asking for a corset or bustier for my fifteenth birthday in three months, but there is no way Mom and Dad would buy me something like that. With my least sticky hand, I grab a handful of cereal and look for an excellent heartthrob to throw up on the wall with the ladies. Timothée Chalamet, Finn Wolfhard, Tom Holland, and the Sprouse twins will be the sticky new additions to the shrine. I love Lin-Manuel Miranda, but he doesn't make the cut. I don't want to kiss him. He's fire, but he is also too old.

While looking for another picture to add to the wall, I see a great photo of Meghan Markle in a monochromatic burgundy outfit from head to toe. I love Meghan

Markle—real-life American royalty. She is a modern-day Cinderella, except instead of cleaning floors before her prince, she was a TV celebrity.

Maybe Meghan Markle should have been the centerpiece of my shrine. I miss being able to consult with Abby. She was decided and confident. I don't remember ever having the self-assurance that came so naturally to Abby. My typical indecision leads me to grow the collage in the closet until it nearly reaches the utmost back corner. I stop shy of that corner, which is too dark and oozes terrible feelings. It feels like the perfect place for a ghost, which gives me chills. I shove the clothes further back to protect myself from the bad vibes throbbing at the rear of the closet.

Still, something is missing from my little sanctuary away from real life.

Do I need more photos?

Pickings are slim, with several pages of this last magazine ruined, dimpled by the drizzle from the evening Abby died. The rain had caught Mom and me as we dashed to our car. We were running late.

I sit back on my heels and gaze at the montage of slick photos. I can't name what is missing.

Tom Holland? No, Noah Schnapp.

As I smear a thick layer of glue to the magazine clipping of Noah Schnapp, my mind reflexively tags Sam onto my mental list of hotties. I begin daydreaming about the mysterious Sam but then my ill-fated love affair with Ethan Thomas comes unceremoniously stomping into my mind. I shudder and accidentally apply too much glue to the picture of Noah. It is ruined.

Well, that feels about right.

Quickly, I cross my sticky fingers and pray things with Sam will work out a whole lot better than they did with Ethan.

***

I clearly remember it had only been two weeks since Abby's funeral when the adults in my life, in all their grievous wisdom, decided it was time for me to return to life as usual, a.k.a school. No one asked me what I thought. No one acknowledged that returning to normal was impossible. No one but the kids noticed I returned to school in my pajamas.

There I stood, just outside the principal's office, in pink slipper socks stuffed into my navy-blue Adidas slides. I had on my fleece Lilo and Stitch pajama pants that I'd been wearing for days and my black *My Chemical Romance* sweatshirt. I stuck out like a roasted pig at a PETA conference.

The fluorescent lighting, the bang of lockers, and the voices competing to be heard were harsh and grating on my overexposed nerves. It was too soon to be among peers and navigating the choppy waters of adolescence. I didn't expect sympathy. I steeled myself for the goggling eyes and winged whispers of gossip. For the first five minutes, my prediction of junior high kids was spot on, but then the horde approached with smiles and outstretched arms.

Everyone wanted to be my best friend, a significant departure from my status before Abby's death. I went from a nobody to a morbid curiosity, a paragon of popularity. But this attention was unwanted; I didn't want to talk about or even remember the accident. I had been fighting to keep that night out of my mind, and this blood-sucking posse of peers was never going to leave me alone. My breathing became shallow, and I shuffled my feet. I told myself I could make it through my classmates' forgery of feelings as long as I didn't puke.

Don't puke.

I tried sinking into the background of the halls hung

with poster-painted signs hawking the upcoming bake sale. I hugged the corners, peeking for safe passage to my classes. And I spent a lot of time locked in a bathroom stall with my feet tucked up. That is until one of my slides plopped in the toilet. After fishing it out, I held it under the air dryer.

But none of these things mattered when Ethan Thomas, the second most popular boy in school, asked me to the Spring Fling dance. I was dazed into acceptance. My mouth was so dry I couldn't choke out a simple yes or no. So, I slowly nodded as the gaggle of nearby girls squealed with delight. Ethan flipped his fluffy hair off his forehead, nodded, and left the girls to oooh and aww over this stunning turn of events.

Twice in one day, I made junior high history.

When I regained my faculties, I was pissed. On top of everything else, I would have to feign interest in a popular boy. *I would have to fake it, right?*

Heck, I couldn't fake my way through a breakfast of burnt Pop-Tarts with my parents. How was I supposed to be a smiling junior-high socialite? I was numb, dumb, and had unwittingly become the class pet project. Everyone wanted to stand near me. Everyone wanted a glimpse of death. And now, my classmates were offering me what I had always wanted: popularity and a boyfriend.

Only, it was all too late. I had already been beaten, subdued, and locked away deep inside an Anna shell.

I felt something deep inside stir and sniff about, seeking out this invitation to my adolescent dreams. *Dare I hope that someone could see me?* That I was more than an echo of Abby? Was this date with Ethan my first step towards being kissed? Maybe on the dance floor, even?

Against my better judgment, I dared to fantasize.

Six days before the dance, I still hadn't asked Mom for a new dress. I leaned against the dishwasher, trying to look casual.

"Mom, can I maybe get a new dress for the Spring Fling dance?"

"Don't lean against the dishwasher. You just started it, and there aren't enough dirty dishes loaded yet," Mom said.

I popped off the whirring dishwasher that was preparing to clean three glasses and a bowl and opened the door to stop it. The machine dropped off with a whir and a clunk. I wished I could turn life off just as easily.

"When is the dance?"

"Oh, next week. On Friday."

"Why don't you wear the dress we just got you for Abby's..."

Mom did not finish her question. The answer was no. I cringed at ever wearing that dumpy, black dress again. When Friday rolled around, I parked it alone on the floor in front of Disney+, watching re-runs with a large bowl of buttered popcorn. It was too much popcorn for just me, but Abby wasn't there to hog it. Mom never asked about the dress or the dance. I wished I, too, could forget it all.

On Saturday morning, Caitlyn Connor called to get the tea on my disappearing act. It sounded like Ethan stood by the gym doors waiting. Of course, since he's fourteen, he only waited seven minutes and then started sliding on his knees across the empty dance floor. Soon, all the boys followed suit, and the girls tried to dance in loose circles, dodging the skidding boys. More than one pair of upcoming Easter slacks was ruined that night.

When classes resumed on Monday morning, I was once again the pariah I was used to being.

***

I push back the bad memory, something I'm getting good at.

Without a picture of Sam, the shrine would just have to remain one photo shy. I grab a throw pillow from my bed and toss it on the closet floor. Kneeling on the cushion before my haute-couture shrine, I pray.

"Please, make me beautiful, give me boobs, find me a boyfriend, let me get my first kiss, and make me perfect." This is my prayer, my incantation, my mantra.

After my vain supplications on my knees, in what I vow will become a daily devotion in the closet, I dig in my secret cosmetics bag. It holds a blush and eye shadows worn down to the pan that were thrown out by Mom. I carefully rescued this make-up refuse from the bathroom trashcan and stashed it away in my Disney Princess fanny pack. I use watercolor paint brushes and Q-Tips as applicators and give myself a makeover. The result is an unbalanced clown look. I'll have to recite that prayer again.

"What do you think, Georgie? Am I getting better?"

"That's what I thought," I reply to the mute bear and head to the bathroom to wash my face.

Looking in the mirror, I can hear Abby's good-natured laughing. I want to talk to Abby or pray to Abby, but it hurts too bad. Plus, I'm not sure how praying works because my puberty prayer doesn't seem to be yielding any results.

Prayers and religion were backdrops to our home's secular Christmas and Easter. Not until Abby died did my family need prayer or an afterlife. I don't know where Abby has gone, but I'm pretty confident that it is me trapped in the afterlife, the life after Abby.

I am sick and tired of crying and trying with ill-formed devotions, so I return to my prayer of puberty. I want to be a glossy photo in a magazine with a never-ending smile. I am peripherally aware of these frivolous inclinations of my heart and shrine. But they are essential to me. I want to be eternally happy, eternally wanted.

My emotional upheaval and inner turmoil are loud in my head and accompany the rush of water, which I splash over my face. At first, my thoughts and face washing prevent me from hearing the rustling in the back of the closet of my room. But the thrum from my room issues a deep, barely perceptible persistence.

I pause, my face dripping wet, and suspect that I stand on the edge of darkness. The darkness breathes deep; I feel my innocence lifted with blooming desire.

Chapter 8

Dead Man's Candy and Death's Appetite

1925

Beverly

EVEN AFTER THE FLU pandemic, death continued to be prolific in our dwindling town of St. Germaine, leaving us neither the time nor manpower to dig fast enough. Samael delivered some souls to the afterlife during this wealth of death, and others he devoured on the sly. Even Samael himself was a tad overwhelmed. His belly protruded like a pout, and he had less time for me. I grew bored of playing alone.

One day, Samael, tired after filling his belly, crept upstairs, seeking my attention. Death stretched his long body, flexing his black feathered wings tinged with a gentle green glow, before collapsing like a telescope into the form of a little boy. The collapse of his wings sounded like a thousand ladies' fans snapping open and shut all at once. I thought it was fantastic.

He settled into the darkest corner of the attic for a rest. This was the first occasion in some time Samael had rested in my company. And I found him even more enchanting than before, with abundant life shining within him while he digested the dirty souls. I was comfortable sitting in this cradle of death.

Samael moved freely about the house and cemetery grounds while keeping an eye on my growing years and engaging in my games. "You count to ten, and I'll hide," I said in what I hoped was a mysterious voice. I was changing. Flirting was becoming on me, and I liked to flex this new muscle. I was getting too old for this game but had noticed the new way in which it was exhilarating to seek out Samael, who popped up in the house's dark corners.

"Then what?" the pale boy with dark hair asked.

"Then you have to find me, silly," I said, shaking my head of loose curls like a halo of gold.

"Oh, that again. Then I win? Again?" Samael asked.

"Then we do it again, but I will have to find you." I wondered if I was losing him.

I dashed off to hide behind the velvet drapes of the first-floor parlor, for I wanted to be found in the dark folds. I wanted to be close to him. Shrouded in shadow the way he liked it.

I was tickled by how weird and ignorant Samael was about the changes I was going through, just as he had once been about these basic childhood games. Still, for all his ignorance, he proved unbeatable at hide-n-seek and alone in stirring a ticklish fever inside me. I never minded losing these childish games, but I did mind the growing distance between us with my pending change into adulthood.

At first, I'd been thrilled to have another child to play with. I'd quickly realized he was more than a kid, more than a human. But he was my friend. He was at my beck and call. All I had to do was call out "Samael," and he would usher forth from a dark corner like he'd been waiting, like he'd been playing hide-n-seek all along.

I was determined to get the better of Samael, so I extended our playground to include hiding in the death chamber, a spot forbidden to me by my father—a location that Samael was well acquainted with. I tucked around a wooden chair with chipped pink paint, the only chair left from Great-Grandma Wade's kitchen set, tipped back behind one of the death chamber doors for viewing purposes. I hid behind the door. It was as far as I dared go.

I knew I was not allowed in the death chamber. Still, something about Samael raised my curiosity about hiding in forbidden places. Samael guaranteed a thrill in the dark.

The death chamber was where my family kept vigil. Sometimes, they waited for days, in shifts, with a corpse to confirm it was, in fact, dead. Then, families willing to pay an extra fee had the body buried on the premises with a bell, to be on the safe side.

Great-Great-Grandfather Wade began the practice of installing scarlet strings that reached from inside the casket to the top of the grave and were attached to little silver bells. If a body woke, they pulled the string to notify they were not dead. While this gadget did save quite a few lives, it wasn't helpful on windy days.

Other corpses, such as John Does or Jane Does, were kept on hand for an extended time due to pending police investigations. These bodies stayed on deck in the death chamber until putrefaction, or until the cases were closed. The oozing, rotting decay usually claimed a corpse before any crimes were solved. These decomposing bodies reeked of cabbage and shit. I wasn't supposed to say that word, but that's what they smelled like.

Samael and I would sneak into the corners of the death chamber and hide, watching Father and Grandfather carefully handle the bodies. But even in their gentleness, the flesh would slip off the bodies that had been lingering or had drowned. I gagged at first, but when Samael was nearby, I discovered I could stomach almost anything.

Together, we bore witness to the shells of humanity steadily diminishing into monsters. The faces of the dead swelled, and their bodies bloated. Their flesh, slack and gray, gave off an inexplicable glow under the light of one bare bulb.

I got used to all this. It was all I knew. But it was my father's hands that bothered me the most. He handled the dead and wiped their naked bodies with a wet cloth. He tenderly dressed them and nursed the dead as they decomposed. Then he would come upstairs for lunch or supper and did not wash his hands. I took to shirking off his embrace, and a distance grew between us.

In a house crowded with the dead and living, I felt alone. Thank goodness Samael was always there when I needed him, although he was always just out of reach, too. I continued to shirk physical touch and grew up a loner boxed up in a house of decay.

Mass graves and being buried alive were commonplace experiences during Grandfather Wade's tenure. All unidentified corpses received a minimalist marker in the cemetery. Grandfather Wade made notches in the simple gravestones to mark how many Doe graves deep a plot was filling up, so he knew how many more bodies would fit. This was nothing compared to the devastation of my Samael's doing.

Samael was preoccupied with me, and that's how I liked it. He said I could see him because I was both touched by death and because I wanted to see him. I don't remember making any choices; I could always see him. I guess it was out of need more than want. But I wouldn't contradict Samael. He said the others could have seen him if they only had been brave enough to face an Angel of Death. I was brave.

I liked this, and in my eagerness, he taught me the intricacies and delicacies of mourning. He instructed me on how to read the tears of mourners and the vagaries of the would-be mourners. Under Death's tutelage, I learned all the qualities of a vast array of tear types. I learned that each tear was unique and beautiful, like a snowflake. With his frosty breath, Samael tracked these tears on the cheeks of mourners, creating a kaleidoscope of beauty on their faces for only he and I to see.

Samael also taught me how to listen to the cries of the bereaved. The deep sobs, the high-pitched keening, the hiccupping cry, the sputtering cry, the loud trumpet blast, the meek and mild cry muffled deep in a handkerchief, the angry rage-building cry, and the never-ending quiet cry that was the kind of broken heart that kills.

Thus, Samael schooled me on the etiquette of death. His greed for souls waxed on as I was knee-high to his glory. And try as he might to ignore his insatiable appetite, it loomed over everything. Even as he fought his brewing appetite, the temptation pressed him to feed on the dead and the grieving. Death couldn't steer clear of those misfortunate mourners, and more bodies wound up in the clutches of our death hospital. And yet, Samael still managed to instruct me on the fine art of listening, something the living were notoriously bad at. I learned to listen for sincerity, guilt, loss, and just-for-show tears in the mix of Samael's mounting hunger for souls outside his purview.

Samael was able to suppress his seething greed for just so long. He eventually took advantage of the living and the dead with an outstretched hand. But Samael's craving was equally in force in my family, who also took advantage to make an extra buck off death. In fact, we Wades had been filling our pockets all this time that Samael was my playmate. Together, we and Samael moved about the sphere of death unchecked. We all moved about with no stopgap, no guard against our greed. My family paid heed to no one and earned a steady income with an industrial and profitable rhythm of burial. As far as they were concerned, the more, the merrier.

I would sit for hours in the graveyard, waiting for a bell to ring, wondering what it would be like to be six feet under and alive. It thrilled me to think of the casket's complete darkness and restrictive bindings. I wondered how long someone could stay alive like that. My breaths became shallow as I prayed for those souls to be taken swiftly by Death. And Samael, invisible to all but me, sat with me among the headstones and silver bells of the Wade Cemetery.

Samael would answer my prayers, too. So, it came to be that no one died at Wade House until I was ready. This was Samael's gift to me. Unspeakable power to name death and life.

Ignorant and innocent, I did not abuse this gift much as I didn't understand it. However, I did not manage the weight of my gift, either. I would call off the bell vigil, having grown bored, leaving the undead to suffocate in their caskets slowly.

And just like that, I'd shift my sights to a game I called pick-a-treat. We would rummage through the pockets of the dead, looking for trinkets and sweets. My favorite items we'd found included a roller skate key, bottle caps, a thimble, and chocolate. One old guy had an unopened box of Boston Baked Beans candy in the front pocket of his shirt. A Jane Doe from two counties over in Sweetgum had a U-NO bar in her knapsack. U-NO bars were the best boon. I loved the milk chocolate and almonds. Whenever I found one, I wore the chocolate on my face like a badge of honor.

When rummaging through pockets failed to entertain, we would sneak Juicy Fruit gum from my father's secret stash on his bedside table. Then, together, we climbed to the top of the yew tree in the center of the graveyard. While we enjoyed our ill-gotten gains in the warped boughs, shed of its dark green, needle-like leaves, Samael would regale me with tales of the tree.

"Once upon a time, way back before the first Wades came to settle here, a grove of yew trees grew in this place. These woods were a sanctuary for many small animals and birds. And the dense grove was the haunt of many benevolent spirits. But then man came and ruined things, as man usually does. He chopped down the ancient trees and used the wood for casks and caskets. He nearly decimated the entire grove to build barrels for aging his wine; thus, the yew tree became known as the 'coffin of the vine.'"

Goosebumps rose on my arms at the ominous name. I looked at the branch Samael was sitting on and wondered at the age of this tree. Next, I blew a big bubble of the Juicy Fruit gum until it popped.

"In man's greed," Samael continued, "the entire grove succumbed to his axe. All but this one tree. This tree was sacred, and over time, its roots drank of the long-buried dead, giving it strength and, some say, endowing the tree with immortality. Thus, the Wade cemetery was born, and people would come from far and wide to touch the bark and brush against the leaves, hoping for immortality, never mind the price to be paid. For it was the chopping of the trees to near decimation that came with the price of death. These ignorant people settled here and named the town St. Germaine, a place for suffering children.

"This very yew tree we sit in, with the protection and the comfort of its twisted branches, called upon an Angel of Death to slay the sons and daughters of Man for their sin. And so, the yew berries grew to be poisonous. The locals, in their ignorance, ate the berries. Then many stillbirths and small children died, which became the norm of St. Germaine."

"What about us, the Wades? What about our dead babies and my mom?" I asked, put out not to be part of the story. My mouth was screwed up in a pucker like a cry was threatening to settle in, and I had no idea why.

"Well, the Wade family was among the settlers, but they deeply respected the tree. They built their cemetery and death hospital on the site of the ancient yew groves because they believed the yew tree gave both blessings of death and resurrection. At first, Death and the Wades worked side-by-side to aid the dead, but things changed, thanks to the piggishness of man. And the Wades were sometimes at odds with Death. To be sure, it was a little bit the fault of the Wades and a little bit mine. Even I can succumb to temptation. And this tree, though protected, shed its leaves. You were just a baby when the first leaves were shed. And the tree has shed all its leaves since then, and it grew no more."

"My family did this? We hurt the tree?"

"No, I don't think it hurt the tree much."

"Can we save the tree?"

"I don't think so. It is in the very essence of Death to stay dead. It is final. The end," Samael said. "But I think you know that."

I fell quiet as I digested this information. I wondered if the tree might resurrect itself, but I didn't ask

Samael any more questions. I wouldn't think of this again until a time I needed to keep Death close to me.

***

The rites and traditions of death were the dance of the Wade House, and the percussion of casket-making completed the ensemble of the lonely song. Like a yawn of death, the creaking sound of the saw produced simple and respectful vessels for the dead. These caskets, made of cedar wood to cut back the lingering scent of death, prevailed in our house in the hopes of cloaking a musty and low-hanging rot. Every casket was painted matte black and dressed in a floral arrangement of white lilies. Anything more would be distasteful.

My father and grandfather constructed the caskets in advance for a standard adult male size. This left the female corpses too much room to shift and knock about. So, Grandma and I buffered the female carcasses with odd scraps of cloth and old clothes packed in with yesterday's newspaper. This restricted movement and dampened the bumping noise when the pallbearers carried the caskets to the cemetery. It didn't hurt that the mourners were usually few and willing to ignore the soundscape of a pauper's death.

As only visitors of the dead ever came by, I was overlooked by the living. But I didn't mind because I had Samael. He was better than any living boy. He was an imp of a young man just out of short trousers. He had bruised eyes, and his affections belonged solely to me—until they didn't.

Wandering into the parlor one afternoon, I came across Samael wearing a vulgar grin of anticipation. He was focused on a bereaved man with a daguerreotype in his hands. The man looked upon the only family photo he'd ever have. His wife and three daughters looked somber. His son had his eyes closed, as did his mother. His son had blinked. His mother was dead. One could feel the grip of death extending from her, reaching out of the image for him. Death always lingered in this room. The grieving man looked up to the vacant space where his mother's casket rested upright against the wall just a few days ago. Then he wrapped the daguerreotype in his handkerchief and slid it into the front pocket of his coat.

I had seen the photo before the man came to retrieve it, along with his mother's jewelry. The camera always captured the expenditure of the soul. A dead woman looked like a dead woman. It didn't matter how much sawdust Grandma had poured into the dead woman's mouth or how much wax and powder she had applied. The corpse in the photo wasn't scary, it was sad and empty.

I turned toward the corner where Samael bided his time and watched. His delicious remembrance of the old lady's soul was smeared across his face. All her life, the old woman had lived under the promise of Heaven, but Samael had cheated her of her fate. Her soul was just one in what was becoming a long line of a soul smorgasbord. I found myself jealous of the dearly departed, wishing for Samael's hungry gaze on me. I wanted to be disgusted, but I was in love.

Chapter 9

Forbidden Fruit of Mother Divided

2021

Cynthia

I FIND SPARKLING MASON jars in the back of the pantry. Why these look recently sanitized is inconceivable. I don't know the first thing about canning, only what I can vaguely remember from watching my grandma years ago. My grandma was redolent with Vicks VapoRub unless it was canning season. Then Grandma and the whole house smelled of okra, tomatoes, beets, and peaches. This eclectic aroma produced and mixed many olfactory notes. It was wonderful. I knew love when inside my grandma's hugs, heavy with the scent of peaches and sweat.

This is what I need: fond memories, not tainted bitter-sweet ones. I will revitalize this kitchen with a refresh and a can of peaches. It is a relief to access memories without pain.

Despite my industrious plans of organizing and nesting the pots and pans in the cupboard, I feel creeped out, like something is spying on me. I make several rapid turns of my head, hoping to be fast enough to spy the thing watching me out of the corner of my eye. I get a humming sensation in my bones that this thing isn't nice, but I hope it is Abby. Then I hear a noise in the basement, a small whimper. I stand on the top stair to the basement, clutching the door jamb.

"Hello? Is someone there?"

Another whimper.

"Abby?" I whisper.

Silence.

Motivated by grief, I react with an emboldened spirit and descend halfway down the stairs before pausing.

"Abby?" I say with excitement.

Silence.

I move along the basement perimeter, looking for my daughter's ghost. But why would she be here? If anyone were to catch me, I would deny what I was doing. I come upon one of the large wooden doors and notice it is open just a crack. This would have been easy to miss when I'd only given this place a cursory glance while hooking up the washer and dryer with Perry. It was the least he could do before leaving on his business trip.

I peer through the crack. It should be pitch black, but an eerie green glow emanates from inside. I shove the solid oak door by pressing my weight into it with my shoulder. I move it just enough to squeeze myself through. I know a response is unlikely, yet I call for Abby one more time.

Nothing.

I can't discern the light source and can barely make out a row of tables. With my right hand, I reach out and graze one of the cold concrete slabs. Briefly, the grime radiates a green light when I bring my hand up to my face. The light pulses and fades. It leaves a fine ash thick with moisture along my fingers. At least, it appears that way in the low light.

I sniff my hand. This gunk stinks of rotten vegetables, the leafy green type that liquefies to brown and smells up the whole refrigerator. I put my finger to my lip and hesitantly lick it. I have no idea why I do this, and I instantly regret my choice. It tastes like shit. I spit on the floor and chastise myself for doing such a crazy thing. What if that was poison? I wipe my hands over my hips and back out of the door.

I return to the kitchen feeling woozy, and time spools out at a sluggish rate. I gaze at the Mason jars and how they brilliantly reflect the light. My eyes are red and itchy, so I instinctively rub them with my fists. I think better of this gesture, but it is too late. I should have washed my hands after coming up from the basement, but I was blinded by the gleam of light dancing off the jars.

I sit at the table in the sunroom to grapple with my confusion. I feel a little lighter in body and spirit, like the hard, broken pieces of myself have sloughed off. I enjoy the sweet tang of forgetting and want more. I wonder why, in the shadows of the basement, a light is lit after what must have been a long, long time of utter darkness.

The source of the sickly green light will remain a mystery for another day, but I sense something unseen, which had lain dormant, is waking. It yawns a wide gaping maw and stretches a long dark body, having caught the powerful scent of my grief. The delectable flavor of a mother in mourning. And the memories of corpses and weepers come flooding back to it and to me.

I find myself sitting on the floor of the little, dark

room adjoining my bedroom. There is no electricity in this room. It only gains light from the adjacent sunroom. As I unbox Abby's belongings just to visit and keep her close, I recognize the remains of Abby more by touch than sight. I hold them close to my face to make things out. I should have fetched a flashlight but am mired in grief and stuck to the floor. My emotions unfold with each finger painting, the weave of a tiny potholder, girl scout badges, and black feathers. What on earth were the black feathers from? It must be an art project I can't remember.

It pierces my heart to think there is something I am already forgetting. I stretch and sweep up the feathers in my arms, then dump them into one of Abby's boxes. I don't want to lose a thing, even if I can't recall it, especially since I can't recall it. I am sure I will remember when this fog lifts from my head.

I lie in the circle of boxes and try to rest, but I do not sleep. I let my mind race in a battle to fight off a nap. Because every time I sleep, I feel Abby fade a little more. I am desperate to stay awake and afloat with all of my memories.

The tickle of an old U-NO candy bar wrapper brushes against my hand, but I swish it away and begin tucking Abby's things back into the boxes. I feel a surge of the weight of this dark room. It is like I am in danger of being forgotten. It feels nice.

Chapter 10

The Binding

1960-2000

Beverly

DESPITE MY FAMILY'S CHILLY reserve for Death ever since my mother's untimely passing, I had grown up and lived comfortably with him. He was all around me, and I thought he belonged to me. I never imagined a life without Samael.

During the 1950s, the family business became obsolete thanks to medical and refrigeration advances. By the 1960s, basement storage for corpses was no longer considered a good or healthy system, even for a small town. The board of health shut me down. I turned to every lawyer, every religious clergy, and then every mythical text I could find in the floor-to-ceiling bookcase outside my bedroom. I had to protect our family's business of death. I had to safeguard Samael. Without a funeral home, what would keep Samael near?

I had lived with Death my entire life. I could not bear to be without him. But I knew I was not enough. I had to find a way to make him stay, to feed his appetite for souls.

I knelt over my bed, digging and flipping through the library of books I'd dumped on the saggy mattress. I knelt as if praying over these aged tomes, seeking salvation. In my frantic research through stacks of dusty books about Death that the family had accumulated over generations, I stumbled across a binding spell. It was an exorcist's spell, but I thought I could combine it with an Egyptian priest's prayer and mold it to my needs. It would condemn Samael to an existence without purpose. But I could not lose him.

In my sorrow and anger and fear, I failed to understand that I was cutting Samael off from the savory drippings of mourners and from the feeding ground of souls, which had become essential to his existence. He had grown greedy and lazy over the easy pickings at our house and had stopped delivering souls to their afterlife. He'd kept them for himself, an unnatural diet of spirits. St. Germaine was not a good place to die.

I grabbed a handful of gold teeth, extracted from corpses over the years, from the jar in the basement. The teeth clacked together as they tumbled from the finger-smudged Mason jar into my sweaty palm. I had them melted down by a discreet jeweler who had fallen on hard times in our dwindling town. He forged the gold into a cartouche, a long, slender, oblong pendant of gold. The perfect replica of an ancient Egyptian amulet. One side was inscribed with my interpretation of Samael's name in hieroglyphics: a keen-sighted owl, a reaper of souls, an arm as a symbol of power, and a lion symbolizing danger, chaos, and protection. On the other side, the cartouche had an inscription of a Latin incantation to bind this Angel of Death, Samael, unto me.

I took the newly fashioned cartouche and a splinter from the yew tree of death, which still stood as a haunting resurrection from my childhood that I'd once climbed and skinned my knees upon. I gathered my mysteries and lit a candle.

I made a circle of salt just outside my closet where Death liked to nest. My hope was to trap him long enough to finish the spell. Then I pricked my finger with a pocketknife and dripped blood on the splinter and the cartouche. I recited the spell I'd copied from a hodgepodge of superstitions and mythologies found in the faded books. I was a poor scholar; I'd made a mess of the incantations, pinching phrases from the Book of the Dead, the St. James Bible, and folkloric superstitions.

I had no idea what I was doing. I was neither a witch nor a priest. And in my desperation, Samael was caught and corrupted in my misbegotten magic, rendering him a shadow of sloth and gluttony. The spell emerged with a swell in the atmosphere and withered away to a tight squeezing sound that petered out in a gasp. That was it. My magic, like me, was less than. Death diminished and was absorbed into the darkest depths of my closet, shackled in shadow. And there he remained.

With Samael as my only companion in this fragmented, depressed, and deficient state after the closing of Wade Death Hospital and Funeral Home, I sheltered under the slip of a shadow of Death. The young man Samael was rendered into obscurity, never leaving the darkest corner in the closet of my room. He was bound to me and this space.

He was restless in the shadows; I could hear the rustling of his confines. I found solace in Death's squirming imprisonment much more than I ever did with anything life had to offer. And this is how I lived for the remainder of my years. For Death did not overlook me. In fact, Death became the only one to see me and be my complement.

As my end neared, I was determined to have as many of the rights and rituals that belonged to the dead. I was the last Wade. I cut my hair and weaved my last wreath. I took my time, and the wreath displayed the few remaining blonde curls of my youth with the white hairs of old age. The weave was fine, and the color difference was subtle. My gnarled knuckles braided a ring of flowers for myself and of myself. I inserted the intricate wreath into the last glass dome frame. With shaky hands, I pinned and glued everything in place. Judging my work to be a little wispy, I forgave my hands their limited, arthritic restraints.

Death had been quiet during the construction of the wreath. He had not even raised praise or complaint about my tedious efforts. Before the binding, Samael had been quite chatty and opinionated. Tethered to me, Samael had starved and was reduced to a silent, unseen thing.

Chapter 11
Hanging by a Thread

2021

Anna

THE ROOM IS DARK when I wake but lighter than in the dead of night.

What was that?

I don't wait for an answer to that thought, and I roll over to fall back asleep. However, sleep washes away like make-up remover on a goth girl—smeary, but with a little effort, it fades to a gray smudge. I open one eye and estimate the hour to be early in the morning because of the minimal light spilling across the open threshold. A green light seeps in from the unfinished, east-facing room.

I toss and turn, but an incessant scratching sound drives me nuts. The inconsistent and panicked effort of the scratching keeps me on pins and needles for the next percussive scrape.

What the hell is that?

I sit up in bed. The room is swollen with sinister intent. The clumpy, bumpy half-hung wallpaper frames the room and swells like the walls are closing in and, at the same time, magnifies the decomposing nature of the space. The half-papered walls heave as if breathing. They flex with a long-drawn inhale followed by a labored exhale bowing the walls. I rub my eyes. The walls again stand stagnant and ugly. I and my IKEA bed and nightstand are mere flotsam tossed aside in this overly large room.

I huddle within the scant safety of my white stick-like furniture, a tangle of kindling pushed against a windowless wall. The furnishings and I are out of place in this dark space, with the bulging chifforobe just three feet beyond the foot of my bed.

Has it grown bigger?

Its bulking stature commands the room's attention. I close my eyes and listen. Sure enough, that scratching sound returns like something clawing for purchase. Oh God, I hope against hope it isn't a mouse or, worse, a monster. I clench my purple chenille comforter. The tight-fitted ribbed rows of softness cushion me against my imagination's frightening throws, making a protective and crumpled defense in my fists.

Where is that frantic scratching coming from?

I whisper Enoch's name, but the cat does not show up. His name hangs from my chapped lips, and my voice fails. Fear strangles me, keeping me from hollering for Enoch again. I don't want the monster to hear my fearful, lonely cry.

The scratching grows more insistent and louder. I release my death grip on the comforter and grasp Georgie instead. Then I roll onto my stomach and peek over the edge of the bed. I gradually lower myself over the edge and stretch down until my hair sweeps the floor. Tipped over like that, blood rushing to my head, I look under the bed. Nothing.

Then I hear the scratch again and jerk up. The sudden rise dizzies me. However, this time, I pinpoint the origins of the sound as coming from the chifforobe. Something horrible is inside.

With what courage, I don't know, but I climb out of bed, trailing the sheet and purple chenille comforter. I have Georgie tightly bound under my left arm as I come to stand before the chifforobe. On the day we moved in, Mom had pulled and twisted the lock, but the door had not opened. All at once, I am inspired by why the door would not open. Mom did it wrong; more than that, she was the wrong person. I don't know how I know this, but I am as sure of it as I am sure I like chocolate. I place my fingers against the warm glow of polished wood and push.

The door pops open as easily as that.

When the door swings wide, I am ready to seize the source of the scratching and trap it in the blanket. But a dead rat hangs by a tiny noose from the clothes bar inside the chifforobe. It sways a little like a yo-yo unwound. I have no trouble finding my voice now. I run screaming from the room in search of my mom. My feet make a dull thud as I pump my legs furiously in an exit; accidentally, I drop Georgie on the floor in front of the chifforobe, a mute and motionless guard.

Mom digs about on the first floor for something suitable to battle a dead rat. She settles on a broom and hopes the rat is indeed dead. Together, we tread carefully up the stairs to my room as if a dead rat could pounce on us at any time. We approach the slightly swinging door of the chifforobe, and Mom pushes the door back with the broom's bristles. She jerks backwards. The dead rat still hangs in the chifforobe.

Mom has never been this close to a rat before and

steels herself by clutching the broom tight. While Mom digs her nails into the old broom handle with faded red paint, which she found in the kitchen pantry, I jump onto the bed and stand with the blankets pulled over my head. I shift my weight from foot to foot like I am a dancing ghost or really have to pee.

"But I don't understand. How did it get in here? Like that?" Mom says.

I drop the blanket from my face and watch as she reaches out and grasps the vile creature. Its fur is brown flecked with gray. Mom touches the rat's pink nose and pulls her hand back, her words barely above a whisper declaring it is still warm. The worm-like tail hangs slack. This rat has only recently been claimed by death. Mom glances over at me. Surely, she isn't doubting my story?

How could she? Look at me, so frightened and disgusted. But then I realize her point of view. Who recently had access to the house? Who could have caught a rat? Who knew how to tie a noose? Why? And how did they know how to open the chifforobe door?

"How did you find the dead rat? Why weren't you sleeping?" she says with a bit too much accusation for my liking.

"I was sleeping, and I woke up because of the scratching sound. I looked everywhere, but then I could tell it came from there," I say, pointing at the chifforobe. "The scratching must have been its struggling. Ewww."

"How did you get it open?" Mom sounds more confused than alarmed this time.

"Easy. I pushed instead of pulling."

I do not appreciate Mom's skepticism, but I chew on that bit of inspiration that came out of nowhere. How had I suddenly known how to open the chifforobe? This gives me a chill, and I drag Georgie back onto the bed.

Mom glances away. I can tell she doesn't trust herself to have a poker face this early in the morning. She surveys the room, then borrows my scissors from the floor in front of the closet. "This is a bad place to keep scissors. Someone might step on them."

"Sorry," I mumble into Georgie's pink plush head.

"Fetch me one of those empty boxes," Mom says.

I fetch a box and jump back on the bed, where I'm capsized by a memory.

***

From my old bed in our old house, I caught glimpses of Mom, who busied herself with the back and forth, the push and drag of vacuuming. Mom worked her way down the hall, in and out of the bedrooms. Abby and I were jumping up and down on my bed. We tried to be sneaky and get our jumps in under Mom's radar. So, we bounced between Mom's passes with the vacuum and used the roaring sound to muffle our giggles and game. The goal was to try and out-jump each other. We each strived to make the greatest bell-shaped parachute of our nightgowns in the descent. We made faces at ourselves in the mirror and admired our fleeting falls.

Abby wore her pink unicorn nightgown with ruffles at the hem. I had on my favorite mint green nightgown with the smocking on the chest. I liked how the silky polyester billowed and brushed with a tickle against my skin. I thought it made me look grown-up. When we sat on the floor in front of the TV, watching our bedtime movie, I slid the fabric up and down my shin or rolled it between my fingers. It was an acceptable fidget, unlike when I repeatedly tapped out a song with my fingers on the dinner table.

The bed left little wiggle room for the two of us to

jump, but we were careful not to bump heads or fall off. However, Georgie was not so lucky. When we came down in unison, it sent Georgie sailing, and he smacked the wall with a great *crack*. Abby rescued him from the floor and found half his nose had broken off. A small brown shard of plastic rested in the doorway. Abby burst into tears.

"Don't cry, Abby. I'll fix it."

"What are you two doing in there?" Mom called out from the end of the hall. She knew full well what we were doing, but she didn't mind. Mom liked the giggles that broke the vacuum sound barrier.

"Nothing," we sang out in unison.

I got the super glue from Dad's toolbox. Abby held Georgie still while I glued and bandaged Georgie's head. When Mom finished vacuuming, she asked what had happened to Georgie.

"He's back from war," Abby said seriously, her brow furrowed.

A few days later, Abby removed the bandages. The glue did not hold. The broken piece was missing, and Georgie was left with half a nose.

***

Standing on my bed solo, holding the half-nosed Georgie, my reality skewers my memories and leaves me isolated. I recall the feeling, the promise of youth that Abby and I would live forever. Now, such thoughts seem woefully immature. Whatever painted my childhood with myths of Santa Claus, the Easter bunny, and youth's immortal pageantry has been replaced with the in-my-face reality that nothing lasts forever.

Maybe, I argue with myself, *maybe love lasts forever.*

Senseless as it may be, I still hold tight to my love for Abby. I feel it more keenly now that Abby is gone.

But what use is a love that cannot be shared?

Mom cuts down the rat, which lands with a plunk in the box. The dead thing is so helpless, lying at the bottom of the U-Haul box. By the look on her face, Mom sees something of herself in this dead rat. Trapped inside the hallmarks of death and the mask of mourning, life is choked out of her, just like the rat. I know this because it is how I feel, too.

"I'll throw this in the trash by the garage," Mom says.

"The garage," I start and trail off. I'm sitting criss-cross applesauce, worrying my silky gown while steeped in the memory of the mysterious boy. I roll the hem of my nightgown between my forefinger and thumb.

"What about the garage?" Mom asks with a shade of guilt as if this could all be her fault. She has been letting little things go of late, like locking a door or blowing out the candles. Candles that fail to snuff out the pervasive smell of decay and shit in this house.

"There was a boy. Didn't you see him?" I ask.

"No. When did you see this boy?"

"During lunch. When I went out to speak to him."

"You spoke to him? Who was he? What did he want?"

"He said his name was Sam, and he liked to visit our cemetery behind the garage. I have no idea where he came from."

"How old was this boy?"

"Um, around fifteen, maybe sixteen?"

"That old?" Mom shakes her head in disbelief. "Well, he must have been the one to play this awful prank. The rat has not been dead long. It had to be him. Okay, that's it. I'm going to take out the rat. You check the locks on the doors and come sleep with me for the rest of the night."

I nearly do as I am told. I want to, but ultimately, I refuse to go down into the basement to check those doors. Instead, I lock the entrance to the basement from the kitchen. I am freaked out a little but not frightened. I mean, I haven't been scared in a long time. I am usually too numb since we lost Abby. My rolling disinterest in life makes feeling anything so real as fear difficult. But the rat seems to have broken through all of that. I finally have an intense emotion to bring me back to the land of the living, where dead rats and home invasion wake me from my grief, if just for the night.

I have not slept with my parents since I was little. As a young child, I slept with my parents every night. Then, when Mom was pregnant with a big bump of Abby, I finally had to sleep in my big girl's bed with cold sheets and no cuddles. It was the first time I ever had to be brave. Could I do it again?

Chapter 12

Death Calls

2014

The Ghost of Beverly

MINE WAS A COLD room in winter and a hot room in summer. The insulation crumbled in the attic. For me, it was an all-in-one space: living room, bedroom, and dining room, as I had shut off most of the house with the closing of the death hospital. I only stepped from the room to use the small adjacent half bathroom, which included an old toilet with orange and black rings in the bowl and the stink of years of urine. There was a simple sink with the plumbing exposed and a fogged mirror. I paused in front of it and could make out just enough in the lower right corner of the mirror to see my looks had fled. I brushed back the vulnerable, aged hair with my wrinkled hand. It was more brittle than my hair wreath leaning against the bedroom wall. My apple cheeks had dropped to my chin, which had doubled.

I was ancient at 103 years old. I was puzzled as to why so many women feared death. Death brought mercy and picked you from the clutches of time. When these thoughts framed themselves in my mind with a clarity I hadn't known in decades, I knew it was time.

For a limited juncture, meals had been delivered thanks to a good Samaritan who took a passing interest in the house. But when I stopped being able to go downstairs to retrieve the meals, the service eventually stopped. The mound of uneaten meals rotting on the front porch created a new stench laid over the decay of packed-away death. A foul odor that kept everyone away except a family of opossums with raw-clawed feet. Their scratching on the wooden porch made a brittle accompaniment to the background of my ragged breathing.

At first, I thought someone would come looking for me, at least for my body, but no one came. It was all the same for me, being ignored by the living. I aged alone, unable to leave this house, for I could not give that unseen thing a chance to escape. Once I captured him, decades back, I gave my life to keeping it trapped.

In the early summer, my body passed away.

I was sitting in the faded blue wingback chair, smoking my last cigarette. I'd smoked like a chimney when I was first locked down in this room, with boxes filled with cartons of cigarettes stored in the closet next to the chifforobe. Over the years, I tried to cut back on my smoking to stretch out the stockpile. I was down to my last pack.

The threadbare upholstery of the wingback chair rolled under my crooked fingers. The fabric tore away from the cushion due to an accidental cigarette burn. Napping and senility did not make safe companions for smoking. The burn left a peek inside the chair, the thin and tattered cushion, the rickety internal wooden framework, and the lumpy coiled springs in the seat.

The chair was positioned to look out the high dormer window. This view was tainted by old rain spots and curled leaves. The debris of nature spent.

Since the botched binding with Samael, I would watch for the clouds to pass. There were no clouds on that day or any other day at Wade House since then. Day after day, the sky was a bright, sunny blue—something I came to loathe over time. A never-ending blistering heat in summer and an unforgiving bleakness in winter. It was always high noon, or so it seemed; time marched unwaveringly on yet never changed. I found myself imprisoned by more of the same, day after day, until the day I gratefully died.

That was a great day. Something finally happened.

I slipped off the amulet and put the necklace in a drawer inside the chifforobe, along with my journal and the unfinished last pack of Camels. The monstrous chifforobe had been with my family for as long as I knew. Once the thing came to the second floor, it never moved again. The chifforobe was big enough to fit two full-grown men and even heavier as it was made of yew. Notes of cat urine, common to yew wood, had long since faded to a faint stinking odor that remained inside it, covered by the stale stench of my decades-long smoking. The odor grew in intensity with the increased and stifling moisture in the room that promised a hard summer's rain but never delivered.

That day, the stench in my room was sweet like apples and gross like a fresh shit. I knew it to be the smell of death.

I sat down in my once fine, now soiled chair and waited for Death. I sensed Death awakening. It stirred. It was a starving monster escaping from the shadows, a crippled inky thing that scaled across the floor, making its way to the blue chair and me. My old friend.

Death sucked my soul from my aging body—slowly. He wanted to savor the flavor of his most hated enemy and the love of his eternal life. Death was hungry, and he devoured me in the end, leaving but a scrap. Then Death retreated and receded into the shadows of Wade House once more.

An ambitious real estate agent discovered my corpse, where a small morsel of my soul remained in the slumped jumble of bones with the flesh in decay. Only the fabric of my simple nightgown kept my skeleton in place. My eyes were closed. The real estate agent mumbled thanks. He didn't think he could have taken a pair of pupils staring back at him. He ran his hands over the chifforobe, wondering at its value. He tried to jimmy the lock on the chifforobe door, but it wouldn't budge.

The agent tried to call back to his office, but he couldn't get any reception. So, he stepped on the landing and tested for a signal there but had no luck. Distracted by the old books gathering dust on the bookcase, he eyed the possibility of making extra money. These books were so old they must be worth something to a collector. He picked one at random. In his hands, he held a tome on how to speak to the dead. He shivered, followed by a sneezing fit from all the dust made airborne due to his shuffling disruption of the antique books. He exited the second floor, then the house. He had to drive down the derelict street, six miles away, to get a signal to call in the authorities and a buyer for all the house's antiquities and junk.

Wade Boulevard, the road leading to the Wade House, was a barren pot-hole-pocked blacktop road that ended in a gravel drive and a straggling plot of weeds. A crooked and cracked sidewalk paved the way to what was once my lonely house. The sprawling property contained a detached one-car garage, a narrow yard with a brick oven pit, and an overgrown graveyard behind the garage. The property was boxed in with a collapsing chain link fence. It was the kind of property only an eclectic nut would be interested in.

The real estate agent cleared debris off the front porch and walked back 500 yards to take a picture of the broken-down pile of bones that used to be a house. The house was roomy; that was the best thing to be said about it.

My remains were interred in the graveyard out back, that little bit of soul still clutching to my bones, begging to be spent. But Death had turned vengeful and would not free or finish me completely. The agent bothered to have a tombstone set in the sinking earth with my name to ward off any bad mojo from my spirit. Tombstones don't work like that, but what the hell did he know. He didn't think of himself as superstitious, but this listing made every hair on his neck stand on end, especially when the wind whispered through the boughs of the yew tree.

When the real estate agent listed the house with that single picture, he made the most of the expansive property size to garner the attention of someone needing a bargain. It would take seven years before this house saw another soul.

Chapter 13

Smokescreen

2021

Anna

THE CHIFFOROBE RECEIVES A good disinfection after the rat episode from the wee morning hours. I wear yellow rubber gloves too big for my hands and use a spray bottle of watered-down Pine-Sol. The fresh pine scent makes a valiant effort to mask the stale cigarette stench in the chifforobe. I don't know if this is the right cleanser to clean away rat cooties, but I have to work with what we have. After the cleaning, I plan to polish the wood to keep its glow. I can't say why; something compels me to be protective over this bulky piece of furniture from another time.

This is my first chance to take a good look inside the chifforobe. A narrow section for hanging clothes is empty now that the rat has been disposed of. A small rectangle of floor space is ostensibly meant for shoes. And there are three deep-set drawers. I will need a stool to see inside the top drawer. I consider leaving this drawer alone but decide to meet the obstacle head-on—rather unlike me. I have been trying hard not to be a quitter. This is my fresh start resolution. Plus, I don't want any more dead rat surprises lurking inside. I fetch the stool from the unfinished room, which is rapidly becoming a catchall for cleaning and DIY tools. The wallpaper goop has spread and touched all the supplies in that room. None of my mom's attempts to make this house a home is coming off without a catch.

Today, after putting out rat poison in the corners, Mom plans to try her hand at canning. Earlier, we plucked peaches from the tree lost in the shadows at the house's edge. I am amazed that the tree bears any fruit, much less these globes that drip with juice when I take a bite. When the basket is full, it is hard to tell if we've eaten or harvested more peaches. The nectar still dribbling down my chin, we leave a pile of peach pits on the dark soil.

Before I go to clean the chifforobe, I watch as Mom washes the sticky fruit. She submerges the fruit in scalding water and then peels the fuzzy skin before she fills Mason jars with dark peaches. The peaches are endlessly syrupy. The juice that drips from Mom's fingers coats the outside of the jars. A frenetic Mom races against the clock to can the overripe peaches before they develop rot.

I settle the stool in front of the chifforobe and listen to the cacophony rising from the kitchen, a thunking, deep metallic tone with the tinkling of glass. This steady humming and chiming signals the only homey thing about this house. The peaches' fragrance permeates the second floor and comes to hang with a sickly-sweet hint in the attic's eaves. My stomach replies with a grumble. I can't tell if it is a grumble to eat more or if I've already eaten too much.

Still armed with Pine-Sol, I climb the stool, rip open

the top drawer, and spray aggressively inside. Then I peek over the edge. The top drawer of the chifforobe is empty of anything exciting, not even dust. The second drawer bears the same emptiness. But when I wipe out the bottom drawer, my fingers stumble across a tiny protrusion in the back panel.

With some prodding, I reveal a false bottom to the drawer. Opening it, I find a half-pack of Camel cigarettes. I stop cleaning. This explains the heavy cigarette stench clinging to the chifforobe. Yet, I think it odd for the smell of stale cigarette smoke to linger for so long and so strongly from only a few cigarettes.

How much did this person smoke in here?

I sniff the pack. There is a curious whiff of raisins. I have heard a lot about the disgusting habit of smoking and how horrible it is for your health. I don't recall anyone saying anything about a hint of raisins. I hate raisins. I know I should throw the pack away, but I don't. Instead, I stuff the hard pack of Camels in the back pocket of my jeans. My oversized "Free Britney" t-shirt hangs over the lumpy bulge. This act of rebellion settles nicely about my shoulders, a welcome weight with the anticipation of crossing a line and telling a lie.

I figure if the candle covered the stink of the cigarettes once, it could do it again. The perfect lie hatches in my mind. I will tell Mom the cigarette stench is back, true. Then I'll ask about the matches and bingo—I am in business for smoking.

I skip downstairs and bounce into the kitchen to bluff Mom. Wrapped up in my own world, I barely note Mom's deterioration. Even if I had been paying attention to anything other than what I wanted, I wouldn't have thought a further decline possible. Mom has already been in a fragile state for some time. Instead of truly seeing Mom, I see only the cleaning and canning in the confines of the oppressive kitchen as signs of her trying. It is enough for me.

Mom is trying to give this old house a new life and rekindle life in the family. But my stubborn childishness allows me to be fooled by Mom's good intentions. I watch as Mom dances about the kitchen with jars, tongs, and prepped peaches. She nestles the filled jars in a boiling water bath. Her efforts are filling all the empty spaces on the counter. She is frantically canning the peaches, but the fruit is aging too fast. The rot started the moment we plucked them from the tree. Now, Mom moves like a dancer out of step. She has a few jars half-filled with peaches and other jars jam-packed. The sealing step threatens to come undone and shatter her attempts to contain her grief.

She is sinking, tainting the surrounding air with the sickeningly saccharine taste of death. The boiling water, the muggy air, and her singing suffocate her and me. She is singing "Would You Like to Swing on a Star" under her breath. It was my and Abby's favorite song. It takes me back.

***

Mom hummed "Would You Like to Swing on a Star" while knitting a large blanket in a rainbow of colors like Joseph's Technicolor Dreamcoat. My favorite musical.

"Can I learn?" I asked.

"Sure, ten years old is old enough. Come sit next to me," Mom said.

I sat down with a flump on the couch.

"These are wooden knitting needles. Now, you want to hold them like this," she said as she took my hands in her own and showed me how to handle the needles. "Side note: These are not for fighting with your sister."

"I know," I moaned.

"Now, you need to pick a color," she said, smiling.

"I want to do a rainbow like you."

"Well, we have to start with one color. What color will that be?" Mom asked.

"I want purple."

"Of course you do. Okay, now we will learn how to cast on and cast off. And I'm going to learn a thing or two myself by teaching you. This will be fun." Mom watched my efforts. "Excellent, Anna. You're a natural."

"And when Abby gets older, can I help you teach her?"

"Definitely, you're a great big sister!" Mom said.

I liked making rows of loops with the soft wool yarn. And I liked the way Mom didn't mind taking a break from her knitting to watch and guide me. I nestled closer to Mom, making it hard for her to knit because I crowded her elbow. Together, we sang our favorite song.

***

Mom makes eye contact with me over the steaming pots. The look isn't friendly, and her singing stops. I am dealt a harsh blow when I realize this song is not for me, just like the shock and sting of having the wind knocked out of me that time when I fell off the jungle gym. The wind is knocked out of me now. But this time, Mom does not race to my side. The family ditty belongs to Abby now, just like our mom does.

On the surface, Mom's energy seems industrious, but a frenzied quality about her makes her actions sinister. Finally, I can see Mom is stretched thin. I think twice about my scam for the matches. Still, I have got the idea to do this, and I won't let go. I'm not a quitter. I'm about to be a liar, but I'm no quitter.

As I watch her, working up the nerve, I realize it is

something about this place. It feeds off Mom's malaise. A distinct feeling of profound sadness shrouds this house. Perhaps that was what drew us here in the first place. I sidle on a kitchen stool, look up to the ceiling, and ask for the matches, avoiding eye contact. Nothing. Is she ignoring me now?

My stare now drills into Mom's core with brewing hatred. I can't wait for Dad to return. I am unforgiving of Mom despite her being mired in a soul-sucking sorrow. She is not making progress through her grief.

Is she even trying?

At times, she is stagnant; at others, she circles back to where she'd been before. Even as Mom tries to dig herself out of depression with her efforts in the kitchen, she struggles. I can see the struggle, and it makes me angry. Why doesn't she try harder? But something keeps shoving her back. The ground beneath her is always sinking. She tries to hide and deny the darkness in the dank kitchen. I can just barely see this dance with death. And it makes me boil.

I push and punch down my anger with the world, Mom, Dad, and Abby. I tell myself if I were a better sister, none of this would have happened. It is the guilt wedged in my grief that keeps me from healing. It keeps all of us from healing. Once again, it is all my fault. I know I don't deserve to get better, and I don't want to get over it. I am afraid that letting go of my grief means letting go of Abby. That is something I just can't do.

There is no denying that Mom and I both have worsened since we moved out to this lonely house. The pain moves from emotional and mental fatigue to an undoing of my mom's being and wasting of her body. And what makes things even worse, I don't care.

The toll of Mom's efforts to restore this house and family is more than she can sustain. She mostly wants to let everything go and move on to the other side with Abby. I can see it. She desperately wants to leave me.

Despite Mom's best efforts, the fruit continues to go bad. The peaches are in an advanced stage of decay. She will have to throw it all out. For every jar of peaches she turns out into the trash, a little more of herself is rotting away and being discarded. I wish she would fight, but fight what? I, too, would love to have something solid to fight, to hit. With the weight of her grief, Mom just does not have the strength to dispel this thing creeping up on her.

Mom lets a hot jar of peaches slip, which makes a terrific pop sound when it smacks the black-and-white tile floor. Glass goes everywhere, scattering into the dirty places along the baseboards and under the refrigerator. A sticky shard sticks to the knee of her jeans.

Mom goes into autopilot and starts picking up the larger pieces of glass. Her lack of energy and care reduces her to an automaton that needs to be wound up. Her mannerisms become mechanical and jerky. Mom straightens back up and walks barefoot across the broken glass. In a fog, she walks right past me.

Didn't I want something from her? It doesn't matter.

Mom needs to take a nap, a very long nap. She leaves the stove on, passing it without stopping to turn the burner off. Maybe the stovetop would take care of things for us. Maybe I won't turn it off. Nothing matters.

Yet, Mom's bizarre episode freaks me out more than a little. If I didn't know better, I'd think Mom had become infected by zombies. A sliver of compassion kicks in, and I slip off the stool, turn off the stove, and sweep up the shards of glass. I use a sticky towel to wipe up the little traces of blood from Mom's feet, crawling along the floor as I follow Mom's steps to the threshold of my parent's bedroom. But I don't have the backbone to cross into the bedroom.

I am so over Mom's grief. From my knees, I watch the sagging blob of Mom lying on the bed. I don't even really want to help her. I am too angry with her for abandoning me.

What about my grief? What about me? Don't I need a mom?

I return to the kitchen, clenching the bloody towel in my fist. Great, more laundry. I don't want to go into that damn basement. I throw the towel in the trash and dismiss the rest of the mess in the kitchen.

Not my problem.

Now, it is my turn. I abandon the hazardous kitchen only after absconding with the matches from a drawer near the refrigerator. I sit at the expansive oak dining table in the sunroom. Without meaning to, I sit in Abby's chair. But there is no one to protest. I close my eyes and bake in the sunlight, watching the orange splotches popping across my eyelids. I sit alone and wait. Then I gaze out the window at a field of nothing.

I close my eyes again and try to will Sam to come to the yard. Amazingly, when I opened my eyes, he stands in the same spot as last time. I jump up to meet him but remember what Mom has said about the unlocked doors, an intruder, and the dead rat. I am angry with her for making me cautious with her warnings ringing in my head. I track Sam as he gazes up at the second floor.

Surely, he couldn't, he wouldn't be responsible for such a dark intrusion.

I stuff the matchbox into my back pocket with the cigarettes and turn the glass knob. I escape from the sulking cruelty of the house to the abyss of adolescence.

"Sam, you're back," I say, out of breath, slowing my jog. "You're never going to believe what happened."

He just gives me a blank stare. Something is different about him. His shirt is unbuttoned at the collar and something else.

"There was a rat. In my room. In the chifforobe. Hanging, just hanging there. I heard the thing scratching, but by the time I traced the noise, the rat was dead," I say excitedly.

"A dead rat," Sam says.

I begin to feel like I'm having this conversation with myself.

What is wrong with him? Was he like this last time?

Dad has teased me about being boy-crazy ever since I turned eleven. Have I failed to see the truth in my boy-crazy state?

"Yeah, so Mom put out rat poison all over the house. And you can be sure she will check all the locks from now on," I say, almost as a warning. Sam's nonchalant mood heightens my suspicions.

Hell, I don't know him. Maybe he is a weirdo. A weirdo with great hair.

That's it. His hair seems longer today, with more volume and curl, like Timothée Chalamet. The brown locks dip down over his dark eyes, his impossibly dark eyes. I am enthralled. Despite the ominous aura he spins, I consider how rapidly Sam is ascending to bae level. Maybe it is despite or because of this discord that I am drawn to him. He just drips with indifference.

He is so fire.

"Tell me more," he whispers.

He shoves his hands down in his pockets and adopts an aloof air, but his eyes are definitely interested.

I have chills that compel me to tell Sam about how death interrupted my family. We sit together in the tall grass, which makes only the very top of our heads visible from the sunroom if one were to look. But no one is looking. I pull the Camels from my back pocket and take a whiff. It still smells like raisins with tobacco.

Is that normal? I hate raisins.

I light a cigarette, and I think I am fabulous. The cigarette tastes so bad I hope I am the epitome of lit because I'm not sure these cigarettes are worth it. Before I can even figure out how to inhale, Sam declines the cigarette I offer him. I continue to think about the raisin flavor and wonder: Are the kids that like raisins future smokers? Abby liked raisins.

I try to envision Abby as a smoker, but I am overwhelmed with a memory of Abby and a Dum-Dums lollipop stick stuck to her bottom lip. I'll never be able to picture Abby as an adult, and now it will never happen.

"I think those are stale," Sam says. "Besides, you don't want to start a fire in this drought. It would rage out of control."

I am mesmerized by Sam's large brown eyes and suddenly have visions of the grounds, the garage, and the house in flames. Flames lick and devour the dilapidated house. Fire dances, jumps, and scales the peach tree. In its wake, the peach tree crumbles, but the flames are alive with a snaking reach into the sky, sending a foreboding warning to no one, pumping signals of black smoke, which smells like burnt hair.

Who set the fire? Was it me? Was this vision a warning?

I blink and return to the dry grass where I sit with Sam. The only fire is within me.

I decide to hold the lit cigarette carefully. I don't want to give up or leave clues that I am a novice. I wonder if Sam thinks that smoking isn't fire. More than that, I am troubled about the fiery visions of annihilation.

Where did they come from? This house is making me

weirder by the day.

This loosens my tongue, and I confess my sins to Sam.

***

It was the night Abby died.

"Anna, put that down. Come on, we have to get your sister," Mom said.

We stood at the checkout at Target. I held up the line, trying to decide between a *Seventeen* and *Teen Vogue* magazine. It was hard to choose just one. I selected the *Seventeen* rag, but I slapped the *Teen Vogue* on the conveyor belt at the last moment. Taylor Swift smiled up at me. This was the correct choice.

"How can you go wrong with Taylor Swift?" I asked, giving the cashier a conspiratorial wink. The cashier rolled her eyes.

"Do you want a bag for that?" the cashier asked.

"Yes, it's raining," I said.

Mom sighed and tugged on my arm to start me moving. "No bag."

We moved to the exit together, and Mom raised our shared umbrella.

"Shit, we are going to be late for your sister. Take the umbrella. I've got to call Susan and let her know we are running behind to get Abby," Mom said.

We ducked and huddled under the umbrella and scurried in the way people think will keep them from getting wet, but it doesn't. Finally, we reached our silver Honda CRV parked near the end of the row. I handed back the umbrella and ducked inside the car.

"Why isn't she answering?" Mom said.

I sensed that I should at least appear guilty for making us late since Mom went on so, but I didn't. Abby would be fine. She was with the Girl Scouts and the troop leader, Susan. I silently congratulated myself for quitting Girl Scouts a couple of years back. I was absolved from having to join Abby outside in the cold and wet to sell the surplus of cookies. On the other hand, I hoped Mom would buy a few extra boxes just to let Abby out of cookie sale duty in front of the grocery store. Well, that's what I said out loud. Really, I just wanted more cookies.

Mom tried to call Susan again, but it went straight to voicemail. She dropped the phone in my lap and hurriedly exited the congested parking lot.

"You keep trying," Mom said.

"This is why Abby and I need our own phones," I said.

I put in a bid for a cell phone every chance I got. Usually, several times a day. This evening made an excellent opportunity to make my pitch based on something practical, not just whining about what the other junior high kids had. Mom wouldn't admit it, but at that moment, I bet she wished Abby had a phone. She was probably frustrated with herself for letting me make us run late. She was likely aggravated with me and my stupid magazine collection. Then, she was possibly frustrated with herself again for giving in to me. Finally, Mom grew angry with Susan for not answering her phone.

The lack of communication was probably nothing, but it didn't feel like nothing for some reason.

"You should have gone with her like she asked you," Mom said.

I had never known Mom's words to bite. I remained quiet with my nose in the magazine, blowing it off as PMS.

When we came upon the accident, her internal mom's alarm went off. We couldn't see anything but flashing lights and an ambulance taking up the middle of the road, but she parked and sprinted away. Leaving me behind and her car door ajar. Elbowing her way through the crowd, hollering Abby's name. This annoyed and embarrassed me.

Jesus, Mom. Shut the door.

I unbuckled and crawled across to the driver's side; I reached for the driver's door and pulled it shut. My efforts got raindrops on the new magazine. Several pages wrinkled and puckered, ruining the perfect faces of my idols. I rubbed my sleeve against the glossy photos. It did no good. I sank back into my seat and thumbed through the magazine, holding it to the vent to dry the pages. I fantasized about being one of the two-dimensional heroines of beauty.

Then I saw the pink rubber boots with the white polka dots lying on their sides ten feet away from where the EMTs were working. I heard Mom screaming a high-pitched cry.

"Abby!"

I lowered my car window and stuck my head out, trying to see. I could see nothing more, yet I couldn't hide from the din of Mom's wails as they rolled back to me. The sound of anguish lifted in rounds, and I tried not to hear the wailing over the sound of chaos. It was futile, and the sound scared me. I didn't want to know. My curiosity was eclipsed by the sound of Mom's pain. I rolled up the window and sank inside my red wool coat to hide, to muffle the sound. I turned the heater up to create a bastion of white noise. The sound of nothing, the forced hush, and the rush of warmth blasted inside the car. I had been aiming for cozy, but the climate in the car was stifling. I couldn't move. I mumbled a little prayer over and over.

"Please, God. Please, God. Please, God."

***

I stop talking. My tale is spent. The cigarette balances a long ash that falls on my lap. I briskly brush the ash away; afraid it will burn my jeans. I look up at Sam. He is interested, no, he's more than interested. He has a look of understanding. But he doesn't prod for more. He just sits next to me and absorbs the sadness and guilt. I sense his compassion, no, it's hunger. This tickles me. I like the feeling of Sam licking up every ounce of my pain and discomfort. It feels good. For the first time since Abby's death, I release just a little of my guilt like the high-pitched whistle on a tea kettle lifted from a stove. I consider telling him more but think better of things. I've grown tired of talking about myself, about Abby. Who would have thought that possible?

What about him? I know nothing.

"What about you?" I say, putting out the remains of the cigarette in the dirt.

"What about me?"

"Why are you here? And don't tell me 'to visit the dead,'" I say.

"Oh, but it is. That is all I do, really. Sit with the dead," he says. "It's a rather hollow pastime."

"Well, I'm sorry to disappoint you. Would you like me to let you go so you can get on with your chat with the dearly departed?"

"No, don't be dramatic," he says. "I like keeping company with you."

That is all I need to hear to silence my self-defense alarm bells. Any natural boundaries recede, allowing Sam to slide in and nibble at my sorrow and shame. I consider the intimacy beginning between us; I like it.

He plucks dry stalks of tall grass, weaves the papery stems, and then cups them in his hand. He blows into his hand like blowing out a birthday candle until a red rose blooms before my eyes. I reach for the flower, and Sam pulls back. He locks eyes with me then hands the fragile rose over. The rose wilts and crumbles in my hand. I am crushed, and Sam gives a wan smile as if he is unaccustomed to grinning.

"How did you do that? Can you do it again?"

"It is all just prestidigitation."

"It's all what?"

"Manipulation and magic. That's all life is," he says.

I slip a few petals that shook free of the rose into my pocket. When Sam looks at me, I am seen. And that is what I want more and fear more than anything else.

Chapter 14
Ghosts Eat the Grieving

2021

Cynthia

THE DAY IS ALREADY heating up, and I open the back door to let in a breeze. I wish I could open the sixteen windows in the sunroom, but they've all been painted shut. The real estate agent must have hired a few inexperienced kids to slap a coat of paint over everything while this house sat empty. The slapdash brushwork moves against the goal of a revitalized house and depicts the only element of this house that feels rushed. Everything else in this house is firmly resolved in the sluggish days of the past. This house can't help but be a stagnant, stifling tomb.

The breeze barely seeps in through the dirty screen of the back door. The trickle of air does not jibe with what I had in mind. Regardless of the dirt-filtered air, I stand in the doorway and gulp a big breath down deep into my lungs and belly. My efforts lodge like a knot in my chest.

Gazing out at the tall, dry grass, I wonder who Anna

has been meeting outside, if anyone. I descend the concrete stairs and wade into the tall prairie grasses that brush thigh-high. A faint chirp drifts on the breeze from the garage's direction. I reach the back of the garage to find the overgrown cemetery. I browse the headstones with my hands clasped before me like I'm nonchalantly praying. I don't want to touch anything. I've had enough death for a lifetime.

Why am I even walking these grounds?

I stop at the three baby angel markers. In this place of dead babies, I am truly welcomed for the first time since we arrived. I lay down under the gaze of the stone cherubs. This place marks a space for surrender. I nestle in the earth, curling up in the fetal position. I regret moving away from Abby's grave.

Why did we leave her behind?

I roll onto my back and lose myself in the vast blue expanse above. There isn't a cloud in sight. Quiet wins the day. Then I hear near and clear, "You're ruining my perfect day," in Abby's plaintive whine.

Every time Abby doesn't get her way, she resorts to this statement. I've never understood what made the day perfect to begin with. When Abby fought with Anna, she would issue this complaint. I smile to remember.

The intensity of the memory and the unforgettable singsong of Abby's voice jolt me for a moment. I wonder where that cry has come from. I raise up on my elbows and consider the stone angels perched above me. I question what I heard. I hope to see Abby but expect to find Anna. There is no one, no one at all, that I can see.

I recline back on the yellow grass once more. I am cleaved in two: living life in the past and struggling to move forward. I cling to the past to keep Abby alive. I lie in this cemetery as I did at Abby's grave site. But this time, under cover of overgrowth, I unfurl like an open wound festering under the sun. I hope the day's heat beating down on my wilted frame will heal this open wound in my heart.

I wait and wait, but Abby does not come back to me. At high noon, I shake the earth from my clothes and the dried grass from my hair. I am thirsty and need to check on Anna, so I trudge back to the house.

Inside, I am blinded by the sudden shadows of the interior. I stop to let my eyes adjust and reach out to catch my balance, grasping for the back of a chair. But the chair transforms from the wooden ladder-back dining chair I had expected, and my fingers wrap around the stainless steel hospital bed rail. The chemical smell of institutional cleaning solutions and the erratic beep of monitors tracking Abby's life signs set me back on my heels. There was no wasting, no lingering on the fringe. I hardly had time to say goodbye. The flat line declared the death knell that pitched me into an abyss of sorrow.

This moment of loss washes over me, stripping away at my being Mommy. I turn to catch sight of someone braced in the doorway. I think it's a stranger impeding my last moments with my daughter. But it's Anna, frozen with a look of horror and remorse.

Perry is missing everything again.

I release my grasp and break free of the memory and the chair. I stand alone in the sunroom, which is growing dark. Clouds must be moving in.

But no clouds ever cover this house. At least, not that I've seen. And I was just outside at high noon. This place is a nightmare of relentless sunshine where sins and confessions are revealed, and sinners are racked with remorse. If one could only avoid the reach and grasp of this infernal monster called Death, one might be able to fight free of its soul-sucking dominance. But all who come to this house are ensnarled in a veil of torment under a blinding sky choking with bad intentions and guilt.

My new home is Death exposed under a hot light. There is nowhere to hide. The cloudlessness climbs, wraps, and warps this house and all within it. Under this spell of stark illuminations, all of my shortcomings are unmasked. The shadows lurch forth and leach from my deep mourning.

And it feels good. I am beguiled to move further down the line of darkness and deeper into the house. Touching, reaching out to the grave again and again, for my heart has been buried since the day they buried Abby. I join in with the scars, blighted with the truth and damnation of man. I am becoming one haunt among many in this wretched place.

I start to call out for Anna and Abby, but I catch myself; Abby's name sticks in my throat. It horrifies me to almost call out Abby's name as if she is still with us and could come answering. I slide down the kitchen cabinets, sink to the floor, hug my knees, bend my head, and cry quietly. I feel small and want to shrink even further.

Anna calls back, "What? I'm sleeping!"

My ears detect the heavy, clumping steps of Anna in those god-awful combat boots coming down the stairs. I sit at attention, and at the kitchen doorway, I meet the gaze of a little girl with an overly big blue bow planted askew atop her curly blond hair.

"Who are you?" I ask.

The well-fed little girl does not answer. She surveys the room and then makes a beeline toward me. As she draws closer, I can make out chocolate on her smiling lips. The little girl has chocolate on her fingers as well. She holds a half-eaten U-NO candy bar in her left hand and looks delighted with her sweet find. Her happiness shines in her eyes with a mischievous glint. Upon reaching the sink, the child swipes open the black curtain underneath and ducks under the porcelain sink. A scrap of her white dress protrudes from the curtain. The peek-a-boo of fabric will undo her efforts to hide and make her easy to find. I slide back the curtain slowly so as not to scare the child. I just want to talk to the little girl and tuck in her hem.

There is no one.

I am definitely developing a bad habit of being haunted by little girls just out of reach. Once again, the sound of Anna's plodding stomp marches toward the kitchen. I crawl under the sink like the child and will myself to be hidden. I hold my breath and wait for Anna to move on. The back door slams shut.

Thank God.

And yet, I don't want to crawl out of my hiding spot. I run my hand along the snaking pipe under the sink. My finger drips with that same black grime and green iridescence as in the basement. I know no one can see me, but I grow paranoid just the same.

Where did that little girl go? Am I losing my mind?

I stare at my blackened fingertip, which hums a low, soothing vibration that tickles. It is a purr, a promise to deliver me into nothingness. I lick the black mold again, and it empties me of my pain and worries. I enter a barren wasteland that tastes like dirt, but it is better than living with the flavors of fear and remorse. Time stretches out like taffy and is just as sticky. I am lost.

When my muscles cramp, I crawl out from under the sink. My limbs extend and relax as my body takes shape. I stretch out long and lithe. The day dances away in the shadows. My grief, for once, manages to be bearable.

This house is where I'm meant to be. It is where I am. The end.

Chapter 15
Hiding in the Closet

2021

Anna

I SHOVE MY CLOTHES to the back of the closet and sit down on the velvet-tufted throw pillow. My nose wrinkles at the funk that clings to the closet. It reminds me of rotten cabbage. But I can't be sure as I have typically avoided vegetables like cabbage for most of my life. The funky odor, or the candle, will mask the cigarette smoke.

I strike seven matches to light the candle and then finally a cigarette.

This simple act seems easier than out in the yard with Sam. I needn't put on a show now. Just as I think I got the knack of things, I inhale for the first time and choke on the smoke. I turn my face into the hanging clothes to muffle the sounds of my coughs. The ruffled hem of a dress I'd long outgrown brushes against my lips, tickling as I cough into it.

It's my white linen dress with a large, beautiful navy-blue bow pinned to the center of the chest. It was my Easter dress from three years back, identical to the one Abby wore. Mom always made us wear the same dress for the holidays. And as I grew out of these frilly frocks, my distaste for them soared. However, Abby continued happily wearing the darling dresses, looking like a mini-me. This sailor-themed dress had been intended for Abby this past Easter, but she died.

Somehow, this forgotten dress made its way to this house and back in my closet. Next to it hangs another dress that still fits but is too young, in my rather expert opinion. Well-versed in teen fashion, I have quite a few views on what I should and should not wear.

This closet serves as both a haven and a haunt. I am most at home in this closet with the altar of the adored taking shape, even with the darkness hunkered down in the back. I browse my wardrobe and focus on constructing a gothic girldom from these pastel clothes. The jury is still out about whether I can carry it off. One thing is for sure, I need a lot more black in my wardrobe.

I ash my cigarette into an old ballet slipper, another thing I had quit.

Jesus, these cigarettes are disgusting.

This does not deliver enough incentive to encourage me to put the darn thing out. I choke on another drag. I like being bad so much more than I care about breathing.

I'll get used to it.

I scrounge in the closet until I grasp my fluffy winter bathrobe toward the back. Here is where I temporarily store my collection of tiny sample vials of perfume. I covet Mom's little sample spray and dab vials, which I had to share with Abby whenever Mom made a cosmetic purchase.

Painting her face had been one of Mom's coping

mechanisms for stress; these efforts quickly petered out after Abby passed. As much as Mom tried to wear a brave face for Dad and me, it was impossible. Nothing worked. Mom had tumbled down the rabbit hole of sorrow. And I felt like I was in hot pursuit of her. Both of us were looking for an Underland that might contain Abby—or a blacked-out, nowhere to get lost in—but we were each doing it alone.

I roll the tiny vials in the palm of my hand, remembering how Abby and I used to fight over them. We even used the little perfume vials as tokens for betting when playing poker. We didn't really understand poker, although we took note of Dad when nestled next to him on the couch as he played on his phone. Abby and I developed our own rules, a confusing mash-up of poker and Old Maid. I manipulated the confusing rules in flux to win the pot more often than I was due. But I was older; the perfume samples should have been mine anyway. I don't know why we had to share everything.

I consider the tiny perfume samples that roll in my hand. Like everything else, these once-coveted perfumes are tainted with Abby's Death. Abby ruined everything.

Once my dresser migrates to the second floor, I will put the little perfume samples on it, storing them in the small basket I wove in a craft camp last summer. Craft camp was a lame activity that started at 7:30 a.m. to beat the day's heat. The humidity swelled and climbed before swooping in like a raging storm, engulfing us girls in a formidable sauna. I had lingered, trying to find a suitable colored straw to finish the geometric pattern I worked on in the dauntless heat. The other girls were limp under the pavilion, fighting for space before the rotating fan, ready to go home. But I would not be defeated, and I finished my basket despite the heat and whining that encircled me. It was one thing I didn't quit.

As the basket remains in a box, the pocket of my bathrobe will have to do. I grab a Kate Spade Live Colorfully sample and spray the closet to cover the cigarette stink. I spritz around the shrine to cover up the pungent, earthy, meaty odor of mold that clings to this space. I hope to keep the darn decay smell from returning, but the rot will not be eliminated.

I notice a new odor has wormed its way into the closet. It degenerates into a gagging, acrid essence of rotten eggs and mothballs. This stench is similar to the smell wafting up from the basement, which eeks through the crack at the top of the basement stairs and seeps into the kitchen. Drifting across the floor and scaling the walls, it trails a decidedly lousy smell for a kitchen.

I scoot closer to my holy collage of beauty. Then I put the cigarette out in the small dish holding the candle. I don't know if I should quit smoking or stop smoking stale cigarettes. I kneel on the pillow and fold my hands in prayer to the celebrity shrine. The corners of some photos are beginning to pucker and curl.

This wallpaper glue is crap.

I lick my finger and press down on the peeling images. My spit solution will only stick for a moment. I will have to dig out the Elmer's glue stick and give a good swipe over the photos' edges. But that will also be a futile gesture. I pray to God for Ariana Grande's body and voice. My eyes gloss over the pictures of the Sprouse twins, Chalamet, Wolfhard, and Holland. I start thinking about Sam, and my heartbeat picks up. I enjoy speaking with him, but I can't help but wonder what it would be like to kiss him. I pray for patience, but more than that, I pray for a kiss.

A draft blows up from behind me and extinguishes

the candle. The funky breeze chills my bare feet and gives me goosebumps. I watch the subtle sway of my clothes in the frigid breath of the closet. Something cold tickles up my calves and behind my knees, sending chills down my spine. I shiver. I can't understand where the wind is coming from, but I am determined to find out.

The back of the closet seems never-ending. I crawl back farther than my clothes hang. I knock on the back closet wall, which sounds hollow. Likely, there is just an empty, unfinished attic space behind this wall. A good place for a rat to live.

I press my ear against the wall, leaving a cool touch against my face. I listen and knock again. A deep yawn reverberates and replies with a sincere yearning. I scratch at the wall in the back corner. The dry, brittle wall flakes and a scrap of old paint lifts gently off. It floats to the floor and leaves a more significant sliver behind. I finger the flakes and pull off another larger chip of old paint. As I peel away the layers, a crypt-like fragrance blooms all around. The wall beneath the paint layers is merely pressed paper. No wonder I feel a cold draft of air pushing against this tender wall.

Then, slowly, I raise the pointer finger of my right hand and push. Nothing. This time I poke again like I am poking Abby hard in the chest, telling her to go away. My finger punctures the wall and leaves a peephole behind. I retract my finger and then haltingly bring my face to the hole. I peer into the darkness. I see nothing but feel an obtrusive thin air blowing into my eye, drying it out. The chilled breeze makes the faintest whistling sound. I back out of the closet, rubbing my fist in my right eye, and I move the clothes to cover up the hole.

When I retire from the closet, I close the door and

open the chifforobe to return the stale cigarettes to their hiding place.

What else can I do with the cigarettes?

I want to keep them in case I need to look lit, even if Sam has yet to be impressed. After all, they are the only cigarettes I have. I pull out the bottom drawer and open the false bottom—which isn't empty.

There winks a glint of gold, a necklace. The light from overhead shines down, making it sparkle. I scoop up the chain.

Was this here before? Did I miss it in the corner of the drawer, distracted by the cigarettes?

I can't be sure. The dainty chain carries a pendant made of a heavy, slender bar of gold scratched with some illegible markings. A heavier chain would be a better choice for the weight of the pendant. I run my fingers over the pendant, attempting to read the etchings under my fingertips. I hold the necklace up to the window to catch the moonlight shining through the recently cleaned glass, and it shines brilliantly, almost as if it glows from within. It is beautiful and impressive.

What do the symbols mean?

They appear to be a combination of hieroglyphics and Latin. I love the newfound treasure and slip the chain over my head. Distracted from the cigarettes, I drop them carelessly into the drawer. Then I retreat to the bundle and warmth of my bed, where I continue rubbing the gold bar between my fingers. I try translating the Latin, thinking back to Mr. Smith's class. I am no expert, but I got a B+.

This necklace is the second favor from this giving drawer. The Camels had been stale and disgusting, but I couldn't care less. I have a gold necklace now.

I love its weight on my chest and the gleam of its beauty. With the necklace, I move past the enticing sense of rebellion. I graduate to feeling grown-up. The necklace has a magical essence. When I put it on, a deep hum started in my chest, graduating to my heart, radiating through the top of my head, and then vibrating through the tips of my fingers and toes. I am giddy, which is better than the nauseating cigarettes. I just traded up.

***

I am struggling with the sheets and blankets again. Instead of a tug-of-war tonight, I am pinned down under the jumble of bedclothes. The blankets are restraining me and suffocating me. I find myself paralyzed and sweating. I keep telling myself to move, to wake up, but I remain bound under the bed linens. My chest feels tight. The chenille comforter is held firmly against my shoulder, tickling with the pressure. The blanket is tight against my face, and I gasp for air. I panic. Then, with a surge of anger, I bolt upright and toss the blankets to the foot of the bed.

"Stop!"

My anger ceases immediately when I see Abby standing inside the closet. The door is open. And she stands there, just stands there, in her Brownie uniform.

Her left arm dangles unnaturally from her shoulder, dislocated and broken. Abby's face is scarred with road rash. Her mauled raw flesh reminds me of uncooked hamburger meat or Sloppy Joe Day at the school cafeteria. This makes me nauseous. Abby's skull is sunk in on the left side, and her left ear is missing. I reluctantly speculate where the missing left ear and her brains could be.

Were they smeared across the wet pavement? What happened to these parts of Abby? Were they left on the road? Hosed off?

There are so many practical questions about Death that I have never encountered before.

This gruesome specter in my closet is not how Abby appeared at the funeral. People kept saying how perfect she looked. They, whoever they were, had made her beautiful.

"It looks just like her," the people whispered.

All the faceless people who claimed to know my family pushed and prodded their way to the front, to Abby. But I couldn't recall a single one of them. I understood the funeral was a lie, like a school pageant. Abby never lay perfectly still. Abby was never quiet. She was a bundle of sound, incessantly talking, narrating even the most inane aspects of daily life. She even spoke in her sleep when she and Georgie would cross the hall to my bed and crawl in with me. Abby's babbling was the soundtrack of my life, and now her voice was so eerily silenced.

This ghost before me is a specter of what came before the funeral. It is what Abby must have looked like at the accident scene. It is Abby with pieces left behind smeared on the wet road. This is what our mom saw. I'd have thought I'd be scared to see a ghost, but it was Abby.

Despite the gory truth, I am not scared because I am overwhelmed with sadness and guilt. I cry, and Death listens.

"I'm sorry. I'm sorry, Abby."

My words hang in the cold air. I want to elicit some kind of response from her. I need forgiveness. So, I step out of bed, and my toes meet the freezing linoleum. I wonder why the room has grown so cold, which is odd for the beginning of August. I can even see my breath before my face. Abby has no breath. A fruity scent like apples and berries fills the space between us. I don't dare take my eyes off Abby. I want to get closer but not scare her away. Ever so slowly, I walk toward Abby.

"I'm sorry. I should have gone with you that day."

An overwhelming, sickening, sweet odor keeps me from stepping any closer. A forceful brush of icy air sweeps through the room with firm pressure against my body. It makes a rushing whoosh sound accompanied by the edgy, scissor-like sound of one hundred origami wings. I squint my eyes shut and bring my arms overhead. When I raise my head again, everything has vanished. The closet door is closed. The room warms right up. Abby is gone.

Had she been there at all?

I need to know. I slide back the closet door with one swipe and a bang. It reveals my clothes, my shrine, and a huge black feather. Once again, I know I am being snubbed and ignored.

Chapter 16

A Secret Journal

2021

Anna

I WINCE AT A crick in my neck when I wake up. I hardly slept. I sit at the foot of my bed, twisting, wrapping my hair around my index finger, chewing on the twist of hair and watching for Abby's return. Nothing more happens. I am glad for once that I have no friends here because they would never believe this shit. After the initial chaos of Abby's death, my life has been a relentless systematic surrender, which has accelerated since moving to this awful house.

I am slightly surprised when Mom does not come to wake me.

Lord knows the house needs plenty of work.

I stare at the closet door and wonder if all of it was just a bad dream. I don't want to think of Abby as a bad dream. But I definitely don't want the dead Abby apparition to be true. I am utterly creeped out. I thought nothing could be more unsettling than the memory of Abby in that little white coffin, but clearly, I'd been wrong. Somehow, I have pictured Abby as I'd never seen her. Maybe I overheard my parents talking. Perhaps my imagination ran wild last night. Maybe my mind simply filled in the gaps between the things emergency workers shouted unguarded and the glimpse I garnered from the doorway of the ICU. Whatever the case, I now have more sympathy for Mom.

I cringe with the recall of the night before. My shoulders hunch up and tighten, which does nothing to relieve the tension in my neck. It makes things worse, and a tingling, numb sensation takes hold of my neck and travels down my arm—like a set of metal teeth, a bear trap, sinking deep into my neck muscles. In my paralyzing pretzel state, slumped in bed, I am plagued with the grotesque visions from last night, like lacerations on the backs of my eyelids. I consider plucking out my eyes to help ease the pain and prevent further visual hallucinations. But it is too late; my memories lay like spiders' eggs.

The stark and disturbing reality of Abby's accident has been laid bare. I see myself differently, too. I realize the awful truth: I am not the center of anyone's universe. I only vaguely possess the focal point of my own world, which honestly revolves around my dead sister. Then I wonder whether I have inadvertently killed the only person to truly love me.

I only have one foot out of bed when I hear a scuffle inside the chifforobe. I quickly withdraw my foot and sink back into the blankets.

"Are you kidding me?" I announce to the room. But there is no one to hear except Georgie.

I gather my courage and step up to the chifforobe, lurching like Quasimodo. Stiff neck or not, I will not stand for another hung rat. The scratches and scritches are louder than last time. More than one rat might be loose in the chifforobe.

I steel myself, plant my feet on the floor, shoulder-width apart, and open the yew door. There is a yowling screech, and something pounces on my face. The thing draws blood on my cheek and claws my chest through the nightgown before jumping to the floor. I see a streak of orange leap from my feet to the bed. It is Enoch.

He saunters across the comforter as if nothing has happened and starts licking a paw to groom himself. I spin back to the open chifforobe, but for once nothing unusual comes from this piece of furniture. The looming chifforobe retains its faint cat urine odor and gargantuan size. I press my forearm against my cheek and a thin trace of blood transfers to my sleeve.

How did Enoch get inside the chifforobe?

But no matter how long I stand in the wake of the open door, I can only guess I'd shut him up by accident. This happens from time to time. If we didn't take the time to double-check, Enoch often got trapped in closets. Abby and I called it "Enoch Shopping Time." Enoch took every chance to roam about and "shop" for cat-sized souvenirs in the closets back home. Dad instated a rule that all closets must be kept shut. He'd grown tired and grumpy about fishing Enoch's treasures from clogged toilets. Abby and I thought the whole thing funny until Enoch dropped the tiny Ariel collectible figure in the toilet, and Abby had forgotten to flush. After the Disney Princess toilet kerfuffle, we remembered to shut closet doors and flush.

I inspect the inside of the chifforobe for more surprises. The wood interior still gleams even after the rat and cat scratches. I trace the smallest gouges with my fingertips. Perhaps if I start storing my clothes and things inside, the chifforobe will give me less trouble.

I pull a box marked "clothes" toward the bulky,

somewhat menacing furniture. I finish unpacking the t-shirts and shorts into the middle drawer. Seated on the floor, I'm contemplating what clothes to hang on the rack when I bump my funny bone on the bottom drawer, which has cracked open of its own accord.

Dang!

I rub my elbow and straighten up on my knees to peek into the drawer. I pop the false bottom up and reach inside for the partially used pack of cigarettes.

Too early for a rebellious act?

My right-hand scrambles about the bottom of the drawer, but there are no cigarettes. Instead, I find a book. Gently, I lift an old book from the bottom drawer with both hands. I set the book in my lap, and with my right hand, I reach back into the drawer, grabbing about for the Camels, but they are gone.

I turn my attention back to the book. The cover clings to the pages with loose bindings. I carry it to the bed and lay it down carefully. I run my fingers slowly over the cover. The book has no title, not a word. My fingertips rub the bumps and snags of the raw silk cloth covering, which is a beautiful golden yellow. The luxury of the material makes a sharp contrast to the failed bindings. I walk my fingers over the book repeatedly, loving the smooth yet rough fabric. My fingernails, caked with thick and chipped purple nail polish, make my hand a grotesque image of a hairy spider crawling over the inherent beauty of the golden raw silk. My ugly hand takes me back to a memory of Abby.

***

I had been teaching myself how to manicure before the accident. With painstaking effort I learned the small-scale designs and styles of my celebrities' manicures. Abby, always a people pleaser, agreed to be a guinea pig as long as I used the pink polish. The night before Abby died, I did my best to paint Abby's nails hot pink with a swirl effect. I thought I had done an okay job, but Abby's nails were a little sloppy. My best creations always came out sloppy in the end. At Abby's funeral, her little hands were folded over her chest. Her fingernails were a natural, unpainted pinky color. Someone had removed the nail polish. I was furious. The message was loud and clear: I was not worthy, not good enough.

***

I shake my head free of memory, carefully open the book, and discover it is a journal. The journal is unwieldy in its aged state and thickness. It emits a soft, scritching sound like a pen on paper when opened. The ink is faded but legible. Scrawled across the middle of the first page in lovely cursive is:

Beverly's Journal

Underneath is a quote:

"The question is not what you look at, but what you see." – Thoreau

Luckily, I can read the script as my grade was one of the last to learn cursive at school before it was retired as outdated. Old things, past things, seem to be crawling out from every forgotten nook and cranny of this house and calling me to pay attention.

I remember Thoreau from English class with Ms. Tillman. She looked like a Funko Pop; a little body and a massive head. I reread the sentence, and the quote snags in my mind. It tickles my inner yearnings to shape my fragile identity and escape my grief.

While I can't quite hang my coat on this hook, quoting Thoreau at the front of a journal is a sign of something.

The edges of the journal pages, soft and fragile, flake like old money. I turn the pages slowly and carefully to keep them from tearing. So far, the book is blank except for the first page.

What a silly journal.

There's nothing here, just empty pages. I flip towards the end of the book. On the thin and crinkled paper, handwriting begins to form. One quick swish of an invisible pen, and words take shape on the page.

I've found a way to keep him near.

I drop the book and jump back. The book is alive or haunted. My fear and distaste for the possessed book are palpable, but my curiosity outpaces these feelings. I tiptoe around the book, looking at its edges, nudging its loose cover with my foot. I grab a pillow and jerk free the pillowcase. Like an oven mitt, I use it to lift the journal from the floor and place it back on the bed.

I hold my breath and open the journal with a quick flick. Almost immediately, the same scrawling script sweeps across the page.

I've found a way to keep him near.

The entry is being written by an invisible hand, letter by letter. With a deep and shaky exhale, I sound out the words as they appear on the page. It reminds me of reading a Ouija board. The dark ink presses fiercely into the page as if the phantom author writes in frustration. The sound of fevered writing spills words and feelings across the page.

"So, Gucci," I mutter with respect for the magical journal.

Soon, the invisible handwriting outpaces what I can read. I am, after all, a kid of the digital age. Eventually, I make out the date on an entry:

7/24/2014. The Last Day.

Abby's birthday. What are the odds?

My curiosity is bruised by the ominous date.

Is this journal magic or haunted? What is wrong with this book?

Mom calls for me. I leave everything open and undone to heed her call. Any excuse to get away from this weird book. But if I close the journal, I might find the pages blank the next time I open it. I roll my head back and forth when I release the journal, easing the tension in my neck. I feel loose, and the numbness has left my hand, but the tension returns with Mom's second call from the kitchen.

"I'm making bread!"

Flour hangs in a cloud about Mom, giving her hair a premature gray appearance, feathering in with the white hair that already roosted in Mom's hairline since Abby died.

"You called?"

"Yes, there is cat puke on the basement stairs."

"So? You see it; you clean it. That's the rule."

"So, I'm telling you to clean it. I'm busy here," Mom says. "And don't get sassy with me, Abby."

The name hits the floor with a splat. A deafening silence fills the room.

"Um, Anna. Anna. I'm sorry," Mom says. She blinks rapidly.

But the utterance of Abby's name is lodged between us. The name has been a tangled knot in the family dynamic ever since Abby died. But now, her name is an insurmountable blockage. Abby's name is not just her name anymore. It is an accusation, a rift between Mom and me. I feel Mom wrench away from me, and grief settles in the void. This is not my mom. She is Abby's Mom, just Abby's Mom.

I gather paper towels to clean the fur ball on the stairs. But I stop when I climb down the stairs and see the small pool of mustard yellow puke. Suddenly, I don't care if Abby's Mom wants the puke cleaned up. I don't like the basement. I decide not to do it. The unused paper towels get tossed in the trash.

Retrieving the journal from my bedroom, I go to the front room that holds our furniture draped in sheets. As I walk around the looming furniture, oddly comforted by the ghostly wrapping, I slip off a sheet and take up a spot in the front bay window on a lone velvet chair, another house relic. I brush my hand back and forth across the velvet upholstery, changing its hue and feeling the lush rumple against my skin.

I gaze out the window. The view balks at me, kicking back a busted-up world, warped porch, cracked sidewalk, no cars, no traffic, no living thing. Lost in the scenic decrepitude, I am startled when a page tickles my finger as it flips by. The book now gets my full undivided attention. The pages turn ever so slowly, slipping by of their own volition. Then they stop.

A thick square photo framed in white falls out from between the pages. It is a Polaroid. Grandma had one of those Polaroid cameras. Abby and I found the boxy, bulky camera in a hatbox in Grandma's hall closet one morning after pancakes. We spent the rest of the day taking pictures of each other and flapping the wet, exposing photos like little bird wings. Abby loved the high-pitched whine of the camera.

What became of the pictures we took that day?

I hold a photo of a young woman. I can't tell where or when the photo was taken. The woman stands alone, a beacon of white neatly framed and nearly swallowed by blackness. She wears a simple white dress, and she is beautiful. Perfectly sculpted and almost platinum blonde hair piles artfully high on her head. I have seen this hairdo before in a photo of my grandmother; it is called a beehive and looks like one, too.

Under the photo, it simply reads, *Us.*

Who is us? The woman is posed alone in the picture.

I sit slumped in the chair; my head pressed against the window. I squint and lean closer. Now I see that the woman is wearing my newly found necklace. There is no mistaking that pendant. I play with the pendant hanging from my neck. I run my fingers over the etchings in the pendant while reading the journal. On their own, the pages turn to the back of the journal, revealing a smaller black feather like the one I found in my closet. It marks a page titled:

A Recipe for Life

Under the title is a list, like a shopping list or a list of ingredients. The passage then continues in Latin. No, not a recipe for life. It is a spell that binds Death to life. My Latin is a bit hit or miss, having taken only two years. I worry if my Latin is good enough and if I can use it to bring Abby back.

After reading the remarkable passage naming an Angel of Death, Samael, written three times, with deep scratches on the page and rewrites in the margins, my curiosity is piqued.

Is this real? Can I bring Abby back?

I retreat to my room to review the journal more closely and privately. From page to page, the journal is filled with Beverly's handwriting, with a soft scratch made on the pulpy paper. The ghostwriting has a rhythmic nod that fills my head with disconnected notions, eerily familiar to my deepest wishes. Fascinated but weary, I wonder if I can ever make sense of the memories and incantations in this book.

Can I truly bring Abby back?

Chapter 17
Written Wishes

2021

Anna

While the journal fills with sweeping cursive entries, there are still plenty of blank pages. It is an invitation to write. I hope my entries will create a dialogue with Beverly.

Ever since Abby died, life has become less. Less color, less clear, less feeling, less me.

I write with a pencil, the only thing I have at hand, and it is a relief to confess my feelings.

It is all my fault.

As my feelings soften, they return to the sensation of my chest being placed in a vise grip. I am not ready for the truth, even if it is mine.

Realizing admission is more than I can handle, I try to erase my words, to erase it all. I am foiled. The pink rubbings of the little eraser tip ball up and scatter across the page, but the words won't go away.

It is all my fault.

The curled-up rubber remnants will not be

brushed clear. The text, although in pencil, cannot be unwritten, and the eraser rubbish is much like the remains of the girl I used to be. This old journal has caught my feelings and holds them to the page.

It is all my fault.

I try to erase my words once more, to no avail. I surrender the pencil to the page again.

I am dead without Abby. I am the Walking Dead, and it doesn't feel as sexy as all those zombie movies I used to make Abby sit through. I am a terrible sister.

This time, I don't even try to erase my thoughts. Instead, I hope Beverly might have some advice. I await Beverly's reply in the rush of pen scratches on paper.

I feverishly read Beverly's story: her birth, her mother's death, so many deaths. I stop reading and look at my bedroom with new eyes. Beverly lived and presumably died in this very room. A freaky thought that sends shivers down my spine. I wrap my arms around myself and brush my hands up and down, trying to get warm.

It is impossible to read the entries in order. The free-range turning of the pages obliterates any structure, rhyme, or reason. Obliged to read where the pages take me, my confusion increases.

I assume Beverly is the guiding force in this journal and the woman in the Polaroid. But I also sense another presence, something protecting this room, which has settled in with deep roots upon the discovery of this journal. There is more to this house.

Who is there? What does it want? Is it Beverly?

I'm frustrated with the lack of clear knowledge. I shake the journal, hoping for another Polaroid or feather or anything. The threads of the back binding snap free, and the back cover falls to the floor. I hold the broken journal in my sweaty hands.

What have I done?

I have to fix the journal. I cross to the unfinished room, our pit stop for the miscellaneous. I find a roll of duct tape before being distracted by the morning light winking in the windows, beckoning me forward. I eye the stool and whisk it over to the high windows. I climb up but still stand on tiptoe and grasp the window ledge with my fingers to see outside. I half expect to see Sam. He is in the yard a lot, but not now.

What had he been looking for when he gazed up at this room?

I wonder if Sam has ever been in this house. It stood empty for a long time. Determined to get real answers, I put the roll of duct tape on my bed with the journal. I will return to fix the book later. At the moment, I need some distance from my room and the ghost writer. So, I head downstairs to explore the first floor and the graveyard with new eyes.

I don't know where to begin my house investigation because I don't know what I am looking for. With no better place to start, I search the closets on the first floor. I find little in my search but scraps of old stuff like scarlet string, an old roller skate key in the back of a closet in my parent's bedroom, old bottle caps in the pantry, and a thimble.

I know what a thimble is from when I earned my sewing badge back during my Girl Scout days. Abby had been struggling with this same badge when she died. Since a thimble was a common household item in the old days, it could easily be a relic of the prior inhabitants. Still, I want to imagine the thimble as a gift from Abby. The sunroom table, except for the thimble, becomes a temporary exhibit for my newfound treasures.

I keep the thimble safe in my pocket.

I survey the dark, tiny room wedged between my parents' room and the sunroom. It is an odd space with dim, indirect light and no privacy. Abby's boxes quickly filled it up. I did not expect to find anything here, but I am curious to peek into the boxes and see what of Abby is inside these cardboard urns. I rifle about a few boxes that primarily hold old schoolwork and artwork. I feel my heart open like a flower, but it wilts as fast as it blooms.

Why is Mom keeping this stuff? It just makes her sad. Where is Mom?

I dig deeper. I hold a piece of construction paper with a mess of green-yellow-brown smears. I have no idea what it's supposed to be, but I can make out the streaks left by tiny fingers. I keep digging. I find something odd and intricate. I raise up on my knees to get a better look. It's a wreath under a glass dome. It looks like a wreath of dried flowers, but maybe not flowers. It looks like it's made of wool or some thread suitable for weaving. I admire its detail of little petals and leaves.

This did not belong to Abby. This is old. I wipe away the dust on the dome with my sleeve. There is a piece of paper tacked inside with the wreath. It reads: *Beverly Wade*. There is that name again. I put it back gently. Why the spooky and dull wreath is in one of Abby's boxes is beyond my understanding. I'll have to ask Mom later.

I have one space left to explore, the basement. I stall big time. I scrub my hands, rubbing them raw in the kitchen sink under a veil of sickly-sweet steam. Mom's onslaught of cleaning has heroically battled the stench of rot in this house. But Mom's labor is waning just as the bluing blight of rotten peaches intensifies inside glass jars scattered over the kitchen island. The odor of decay marries poorly with the smell of homemade bread currently wafting from the oven.

How much bread is she making?

I rummage around the counter drawers. I search for Cherry Coke among the grocery bags on the worn wood of the center island. Nothing but bundles of flour and yeast are in the bags. Mom forgot again. Contemplating my next move as I dry my hands, I realize I'm still looking at things all wrong.

I need an outside-in approach, which means postponing the basement search. My shoulders relax, and I run outside. The heavy pendant thumps against my chest as I run. I don't see Sam, but I keep running until I reach the farthest end of the yard.

I hesitate to cross through the gate into the graveyard. The wrought iron fence and gate constructed of serpents devouring each other makes a formidable bastion of Death. The biggest snake hangs menacingly overhead. Its scales, crafted with razor-sharp edges, gleam while it eats its own tail. How had I overlooked this Goth artistry before? It undoubtedly appeared much less creepy when I first encountered the gate with Sam there.

Chapter 18

Prayers to Beverly

2021

Anna

I MUST KNOW IF the writings in that old journal are trustworthy.

Did my room once belong to someone named Beverly? Were there dead babies in this graveyard?

I cross inside the cemetery, pushing open the wrought iron gate. The wind dies. I walk deeper into the graveyard, setting my sights on the three weeping angel gravestones in the center. These stone cherubs gather around a crooked, tall, knobby yew tree with a crow perched on the lowest branch.

Birds. I hate birds.

I fear the bird will beat about my head and become entangled in my hair, pecking and whipping into madness.

***

My severe distaste for birds came from Caitlyn Connor's eleventh birthday party. The other girls huddled together in their sleeping bags with a giant bowl of popcorn while watching Hitchcock's *The Birds.* I thought the movie was slow and stupid. Then Caitlyn's big brother released his pet parrot into the room from the shadows and under the screams of Tippi Hedren. Everyone screamed. I peed my pants and the sleeping bag.

It was the cringiest moment of my life. It was almost the worst accident of my life. I'd been holding it in for quite a while, waiting for Margot to return from the bathroom. Margot had been hogging the bathroom all night because she drank a two-liter Coke all by herself. The event was social suicide for me.

***

Another lousy memory pecking at me; I brush it aside. Standing at the center of the cemetery, I think the little angel gravestones surrounding the base of the yew tree are like chicks cozied up to a mother hen. These graves are not as overgrown as some, but old just the same. Each mark the brief life of a Wade baby:

Mary Anne Wade, Born and Died April 15, 1906

Cassandra Mae Wade, January 7, 1908 – January 27, 1908

Evelyn Bea Wade, October 12, 1909 – March 27, 1910

As the journal said, the three dead babies in the graveyard were siblings to Beverly Wade. I spin in a circle, looking for a tombstone for Beverly.

She must be here.

I prowl, careful not to step on any graves, which is not easy in the crooked graveyard. The graveyard clearly does not have a plan. It twists and turns between graves from the mid-1900s back to headstones from the mid-1800s.

The tombstone artistry runs the gamut from the extravagant monuments of the wealthy to the bleak, book-sized slabs sinking in the ground, waiting to get lost in the overgrowth. But it is easy to find Beverly. Hers is the freshest grave in this cemetery, without weeds to cover the bald etchings, as if her grave were being kept up by someone.

Beverly Marie Wade
June 14, 1911 – July 2014

Beverly's grave isn't ornate like the other Wade's in the cemetery. I guess this is because Beverly had been the last Wade. She had no one to look out for her. I kneel in front of the grave.

"Jesus, she was old. 103?"

I lick my left palm and smooth my hair down. I don't know why I do this, and I am grateful I don't have an audience. I am tired of being under a microscope and ignored at the same time. It is a feeling of anxiety and itchiness. I don't like it.

Back when we were driving out to the house, sight unseen, I dreamt it would be like a vacation from the jury of my peers. I knew junior high was vicious before Abby died. Afterward, my friends and frenemies were nothing more than vipers and vultures drawn to the drama of demise. I did not like being the harbinger of mortality, yet I could not escape the taint of Death. Once the novelty wore off, friendships eroded; then I was just marked with the stain of Death.

Over the first few days here, it became blisteringly apparent that I had entered just another scene of voyeurism and eating of my bones. I had gone from one haunt to another and was still just as befuddled as to how to fight back against a life filled with death.

I rock on my knees in the graveyard dirt, trying to be respectful and think of what I want and need to say. As a C and E Catholic, Christmas/Easter, I was not particularly familiar with praying, but I had to try.

"Miss Beverly, my name is Anna. I live in your house now. In fact, I live in your room. I don't know if you are haunting me, but could you please make my sister come back? I'd really like to talk to her. And if it isn't too much trouble, try not to scare me anymore. Amen. I mean, thanks."

I rise and clap the clumps of dirt from my hands, ready to head back to the house. The earth of Beverly's grave is loose, and I smudged my palms when I pressed them into the ground to stand up. I rub my hands over my hips, leaving muddy marks on my jeans. I am not cleaning up. I am just moving the dirt around.

The oddity of Beverly's fresh grave is not lost on me. It reaffirms my suspicions that Beverly haunts this house.

As I approach the backyard, I stop to look at the house, just like Sam had. My right hand salutes over my brow to block out the reflective, predatory glare of the brutal sun upon the sixteen windows. The house looks like a many-eyed spider waiting to ensnare me. The back door hangs open, a gaping maw waiting to swallow me whole. But the eeriest part of the house is the penetrating upper window, milky like an injured eye with a dead gaze.

I don't move. Sweat runs down my face. I am melting under the cruel sun. I stand my ground, take a deep breath, and wait for a face to come to the dead eye of a window. I bake under the sun and lock my knees in determined attention until I begin to swoon.

I look away. I am no quitter, not anymore. But this death watch leads nowhere. I make my way back toward the hungry house.

Chapter 19

Blackbirds in the Yew Tree

2021

Anna

AS I WALK BACK to the house, a faint breeze blows in from the cemetery, making a sound like bells singing a jeering jingle. I stop and cock my head to the side, unsure what to make of the ringing sound. The crow in the yew tree makes a shrill and jarring caw, like the rent of iron bending and creaking in the groans of a shipwreck. Its call pierces the otherwise deafening silence of the yard and lands gratingly on my nerves. I look up at the window just in time to see a pale face with dark eyes appear. At least, I assume they are dark eyes from where I stand. They could have been wounds or hollow spaces where eyes should be. This must be a trick of the light. I can't tell if the phantom face is male or female from so far out. But the face stares right back at me; at least, that's how it seems.

I knew it. Someone is in the unfinished room, and it isn't my mom.

Who is in my house?

I can think of no one but Sam.

But why would he be in my house? Would Mom have let him in?

I don't think so. I duck abruptly at the sound of a hundred crows taking flight. The flapping wings, beating the wind overhead in a flurry of feathered hysteria, issues a rushing, ominous noise that makes me crumple. I turn back to the yew tree. It is filled with a murder of crows where there had been just one.

Where did these birds come from? I really hate birds.

***

I remember the day of Abby's funeral. A pure white snow that had fallen only hours earlier was trampled and mucked about by the many black figures crowded around Abby's graveside. The mourners made a swarm of darkness and despair at the death of a young child. Abby had just begun her life when it was snatched away. The loss was unfathomable.

I tried to find an opening in the tight space of my parents' embrace, but I was already forgotten. I stood aside and thrust my hands, in the too-small, hot pink mittens that Abby wore on the day she died, in my pockets to hide them in this sea of black.

My tears, like melted snowflakes, made tracks on my cheeks. I watched my too-small black patent leather shoes shuffle about the ground, and I wondered if I had put on Abby's shoes by mistake.

When the priest was speaking, a bird swooped near my head, and I screeched. The bird's wings flapping about my head made me cower rather dramatically. The flitting sounded like so many soft chops of origami wings hovering about. I flailed my arms and let go of a peep of a second screech cut short by Dad. He grabbed me by the collar. I stopped moving. He glared at me, then he ripped the mittens from my hands. He stuffed them in his pocket and released me with an ever-so-subtle shove.

In a crowd of people clad in black like a murder of crows, I felt judged. I stood in isolation, and my hands numbed.

***

Mired in this memory, I turn back toward the window. The face is gone.

Is it a ghost? Is it responsible for the rat? Is it Abby? Is it Beverly?

I wait a bit longer for the apparition to reappear. But the face doesn't return to the window, and Sam never appears in the yard. I enter the kitchen, disappointed, and immediately detect the trace of char in the air. Black smoke fills the kitchen and drifts into the sunroom. I yell for Mom as I fetch an oven mitt. I pull out the burnt brick of bread and drop it with a bang and a clatter on the stove. I turn on the kitchen exhaust fan to clear the smoke. I call for Mom again but get no answer. After a valiant effort in the sunroom, I give up trying to wave the smoke out the screen door and begin searching for Mom.

I run a quick circuit around the first floor. After seeing the face in the second-story window, I don't want to go upstairs alone, but I can't find Mom.

Why has she walked away from the bread in the oven? Didn't she set a timer? Didn't she smell the smoke?

This old house doesn't have smoke alarms, but it needs them. Without a window to open in the kitchen, the smoke lingers like a bad omen. I grab a big knife from the butcher's block. The kind that only gets used in horror movies. I carry the blade with its point facing down, figuring the safest way to carry a knife is like scissors. Standing at the foot of the narrow stairs, I squat and peer up, but all I can glean is the empty bookcase.

"Mom! Mom!"

Naked fear ratchets up in my voice and unrolls about the house. I climb the steps, pausing at every other one to listen. The house stubbornly stays silent. Not a scritch. Not a scratch. I wish Enoch was nearby and that he was a big dog. Arriving at the top step, I freeze on the landing with the large empty bookcase. I strain my neck to see into my room. I will have to get closer, which is a little tricky when one is paralyzed with fear.

Instead of investigating my room, I peer into the blacked-out bathroom straight ahead. I let my eyes adjust. It is empty. I shuffle a few steps toward my room, leaning to the right to look inside. It is just as I left it. Boxes are stacked about the room wherever there is space. There is a pile of dirty clothes to the right of the chifforobe. A pile of clean clothes is on the floor to the left of the open door. There is a lot of washing and folding in my future.

But I can't be bothered at the moment. I steel myself to search the unfinished room with the face. Nothing but the cluttered wreck makes an appearance. It is unmolested by anyone or anything. The upstairs is void of life; moreover, it is empty of Mom. Maybe my fears have all been my imagination fueled by that bad dream. Or perhaps this sinister thing has moved on. Another round on the first floor turns up nothing.

I have one place left to look, and I don't want to do it. I carefully and slowly pull the basement door open a crack. The light bulb still shines in a meek halo over the laundry. The foreboding stairs are slotted, planks of wood once painted white. I do my best to gaze through the spaces from where I stand on top. I imagine a strong hand reaching through to grab my ankles as I step down.

And then I see her. Mom is sprawled out to the left of the foot of the stairs. I drop the knife, which falls between the slotted steps and clangs to the basement floor. When I reach her, I wrap myself around her like a shield. Mom is warm, alive, and waking.

"Mom, Mom! Are you okay? What happened?"

"Yes, honey. I fell," she says.

"It's those stairs," I say, looking at the fur ball I failed to clean up.

"I slipped. That's all."

It was the fur ball. This is all my fault.

"Let me help you upstairs." It is all I can do not to cry.

I help Mom to bed. "Oh, the bread!" she says as we pass through the kitchen.

"I got it. It's okay but ruined."

"Well, this is why your dad is the cook," Mom says. She chuckles and slides between the sheets.

"Mom, we need to get ice on your ankle."

"Just let me sleep for a bit."

I tuck Mom in bed. The sheets seem to be graying, and the blanket pilling in the dying light. Mom has already been a wreckage of grief, but now she is a harbinger of annihilation.

Mom had caved to the nagging chore of laundry. I know she doesn't like the basement any more than I do, but someone needed to do laundry. And I haven't been helping. I realize I need to be an adult, even though I have never been a fan of basements. They make me feel trapped. But this one weirdly is calling out.

I'd put off doing laundry for as long as possible. I pick up the clothes Mom had spilled on the basement floor and clutch them against my stomach as I make my way to the halo of light. I find myself inside the blurred edges of a happy memory.

***

Abby and I ran around with mismatched socks on our hands, chasing each other and playing "Sock Monster." The point was to smother each other with Dad's stinky socks. Mom laughed at our smelly game.

***

I wake from the memory with the touch of something against my ankle. I race to the top of the steps before I plummet into more fear.

Back upstairs, I give Mom a Ziploc filled with water and ice for her ankle. I can't be sure what happened, but I know Mom was lucky not to have broken her neck. It didn't occur to me to check Mom's eyes for signs of a concussion. I'm not a very good nurse. But I'm not the mom, after all.

I grab Enoch and make him go to my room, where I shut the door behind us. I go to my shrine to pray for Mom. Sure, it's a sanctum of celebrity and sex appeal, but it also comforts me. This beacon from a former life, a better time.

However, I now need something more holy than glossy for the shrine. I dash to my bed and pull out the funerary prayer card from Abby's funeral tucked between the mattress and box springs. I always keep it near me when I sleep, especially in this place. I pin it to the top of the collage. I won't risk ruining it with the glue.

I shove the clothes back and drop to my knees on the little velvet pillow. Then I notice the Polaroid in the center of my elaborate paste work of carefully curated celebrities. Someone nailed the photo to the middle of the montage, covering up a Zendaya picture. I recognize the white finishing nail from the tools in the unfinished room. The woman in the Polaroid is graying and aging, and another image is shaping up inside the photo. It frightens me.

Who was hanging out in the unfinished room? Who nailed this to my collage? How can the image still be developing? Who is the other person in this photo?

The buttons on the pillow dig into my knees. I push back from the wall of pictures and hug my legs to my chest. I rub my fingers over the bumpy red imprints of the buttons on my skin. The indentations and redness throb just a little. I suck my thumb and rub it over the bumps on my knees while I study the Polaroid.

I can't say how I know this, but I begin to think the mysterious image in the photo may also be the face in the window.

How many mysteries can one house hold? Is Beverly haunting my room, or is something much more sinister here?

Whatever it is, I can tell this thing is hell-bent on communicating with me.

How do you ghost a ghost?

I pray for the face to go away and never return, whether it is a ghost or not, even if the thing turns out to be Sam. When I open my eyes again, I look at the photo with bated breath.

Drawing light from an unknown source outside the corners of the picture, a man appears in the Polaroid. The other photos in my shrine grow moldy and wet, with soot rubbed across the faces of my heroes. The gunky, ashy finger smudges are painted in slashes of fury.

This petty act of vandalism soils and ruins the looks of my pretty people. Someone is defacing my beautiful shrine. I rip off Abby's prayer card with the picture of St. Michael on the front. I don't want it to be tainted with decay. The cleaning supplies are in the unfinished room, but there is no way I'm going back in there tonight. The pictures will just have to rot on the wall.

I slip the prayer card back under my mattress to keep it safe. And so it will keep me safe.

Chapter 20

Seeking Anna

2021

Cynthia

I WAKE IN A spin as if I'd just emerged from a tilt-a-whirl. The last time I rode a tilt-a-whirl was at the parish picnic two years back. I puked on both of the girls, and they cried. Everything was ruined, from the cotton candy down to their Crocs. At least the shoes had been easy for Perry to hose off at home.

I step out of bed to head to the bathroom. A sharp pain sends me to the floor in a crumble with a wrenching reminder of my swollen ankle. I wince in pain but hobble to the bathroom, where I puke in the toilet bowl. My eyes are watering as I flush, washing the vomit away. The faint orange stains are still present in the porcelain bowl.

Nothing stays clean in this infernal house.

I lie on the cool tiled floor, looking at the ick around the toilet's base. Then I raise myself back to the bowl, where I am sick all over again. I realize my fogginess and vomiting indicate a concussion. Still, a concussion doesn't warrant an ambulance in my book. Besides, an ambulance ride would bring back the memories of the night Abby died. Memories I have been struggling not to remember. I want to remember Abby, my baby girl, not the roadkill she had become. I close my eyes and sleep on the bathroom floor.

When I wake again, I equate sleeping on the tiled floor to arthritic camping. Every muscle and joint aches. Nevertheless, I peel myself from the floor. I wonder about the time and where to find Anna. I yell for Anna but get no answer. The volume of my own voice is like a foghorn resounding in my skull.

How am I supposed to get help?

Even if my cell phone had been handy, the dang thing wouldn't have worked. Perry purchased an iPhone for Anna after Abby died, which gave us a false sense of much-needed security. All sense of security or convenience has been stripped away in this house. I have been walking six miles for a signal to make calls or order groceries, which I can no longer do in this condition. The lack of communication in this house has hampered the progress I have tried so hard to make. I fall into a downward spiral that looks a lot like giving up.

The house is unusually still, with no sound of Anna or Enoch, no crack or pop of the house settling, and no door creak caught in a draft. I am all alone. I don't even have visions of that little mystery girl or of Abby.

I have an intense need to find Anna. Dread creeps in as I call out for Anna anew. Once more, I try to stand, rising to my knees while clutching the bathroom door frame. I attempt to stand and tenderly put weight on my foot. The ball of my right foot touches down on the warm wood floor of the hallway. I am just steps away from my bed, only to fall again. I change direction and drag myself down the hall. My gaunt appearance and slow-motion crawl must make me resemble a B-rated horror movie creature. Lunging out of the shadows in search of my prey. The crippling thoughts are all too much, but I have to find Anna. I have a hunch about where Anna might be hiding.

Sinking my teeth into my bottom lip, I know my ankle must be broken. The pain is borderline excruciating. Yet, I don't care. I just have to find Anna. I squirm toward the sunroom, dragging my belly across the filthy floor, eye-level with the grime and dust bunnies I have missed. All the dirt and filth of decades comes out to greet me as I slither through the kitchen. The burst and splatter of rotten peaches lingers, taking up residence in my nostrils.

I pant as I pull myself up to one of the many sunroom windows. As I suspected, Anna is in the yard again, speaking to no one. A breeze sweeps by Anna, lifting her hair in the wind. I study the animation on Anna's face from my perch in the window. It has been a long time since I've seen my daughter smile.

I greet Anna at the threshold and prop myself up in a chair.

"Who were you talking to?" I ask.

"No one," Anna says as her face tightens with the lie.

"That's what it looked like," I say.

"What?" Anna says.

I am afraid I have been neglecting Anna. Things are slipping away from me. It's this house. It drains me. Moment by moment, there is less of me to fight, less of me to remember, just less of me. I am empty, and the nothingness fits better than the grief.

"Ah, whatever. It's fine," I say.

"What's fine?" Anna says while looking over her shoulder into the yard.

"I need your help," I say, looking for a reason to need her. "I can't do the laundry."

"Do we need clean laundry? It's just us here."

"Yes, we need clean laundry."

I can't explain my insistent need to return to the basement. The laundry is an excuse. Something menacing coerces me to enter the dark chamber and take Anna with me.

"Okay, okay. Stay put. I'll do it," Anna says.

Anna's reluctant acceptance is a stay of execution for me.

Chapter 21

The Basement Belongs to the Dead

2021

Anna

"Have you ever been in my house?" I ask.

"Yes, I used to stay there," Sam says with a flip of his tousled hair.

"Stay?"

"Sure. It was otherwise empty, but for me."

"Why? Why would you do that?"

"Sometimes, we are just compelled to do things. Haven't you ever persisted, been driven to do something that made little sense?"

"Just coming out here and talking to you," I laugh.

Sam does not smile.

"So, I guess you know a lot about this place?" I ask.

"I've poked around. Have you explored the basement?"

He is doing that pinching thing with his fingers again.

Is he nervous? Does he like me?

"No, I don't think the basement is safe," I say, trying to crowd out my crush on him and stay chill. "Does that sound stupid? It just gives me the creeps." I nod a quick bob, looking for affirmation.

He smiles like Captain Hook with that toothy sneer that outweighs the crocodile in creepy crawlies. He is like the villain in a bedtime story, in a good way, a sexy way. I miss reading bedtime stories to Abby. I feel a shadow over me. I glance toward the sky, looking for a cloud, but there is none.

"I think you might be onto something. This house has a dark past," Sam says.

"What? Wait, no. I don't want to know," I say, raising my hand palm-up in a stop signal and tuck my chin to the right, looking away.

A silence rises between us.

I start plucking and weaving dried-out clover blossoms, glancing up too frequently to stare with longing at his face and those fantastic cheekbones.

Why haven't I noticed them before? He bears an uncanny resemblance to Finn Wolfhard.

I unapologetically gaze at him for a long time. I know such a long look is rude or blatantly inviting. But I can't help myself. I want him.

"A penny for your thoughts," he says.

"Uh, oh, okay, what about the house?" I say with a sigh.

"It was a place for the dead. Back then, you could taste death and fear dripping from the house's bones," he says. "The dead were laid out in the basement, in the death chamber, viewed by the Wade family, and prepared for burial before being put to rest."

His eyes, like black water, swim with a hell-bent enrapture. He is hungry.

I shake my head, trying to free myself from the fog

that has begun to swallow me.

"Yeah, right. How do you know?"

"I guess you're right. How would I know?" Sam says.

I am torn between being disgusted with this mean story and being drawn into his dark demeanor. He seems to almost glow with excitement.

This boy is totally Emo.

Is this a thing I can get behind? The moment persists and develops into something unexpectedly tangible, like I might lift it and carry it away. This suspended hope for a kiss keeps everything intact.

Sam flicks his eyes at the house, and a threatening smile slithers across his face. My reverie is interrupted, and I follow his gaze to the second floor. I think I see my mother peering out one of the windows in the sunroom.

"I really have to go. My Mom fell last night, and I need to check on her."

"Sure. But be careful, Anna. Death begets death," he says.

Death begets death? Has he been reading the Bible?

Back inside the house, I lay prone at the basement door, trying to see through the crack between the door and the floor. Is the light still on? Yes, it has been on since Mom's fall. Did the laundry matter that much?

I steel myself against what I have to do.

I take long, deep breaths that become shallow and turn into hiccups. I try to erase what Sam has told me about the basement from my mind, but that is futile. I am tired of being afraid. I stand at attention and open the door with a quick swing.

Standing at the top of the stairs, I see the laundry basket filled with whites spilled across the old green and ivory-tiled floor. The linoleum is warped around the drain in the floor and scuffed like it has seen a lot of action. In fact, the only sign of life in this basement is the history of black smudges dancing over the tiles and peeking out from under the unwashed clothes. I tap my fingers on the banister, convincing myself this is a good sign. Everything is the way we left it. Still, I hesitate to go downstairs.

Back on my stomach, I squint over the edge of the top step and down the slotted stairs for anything that might snatch at my ankles as I descend. With a deep inhale, I hold my breath and quickly sprint down the stairs. I stumble over the dirty laundry, now worse for my black boot prints.

I exhale and search the floor under the staircase. It is partly lit by the edge of the halo of light wavering above, and I eye the knife I dropped yesterday. I carefully inspect the basement with my back to the water heater and furnace. The corners are thick in shadow. The exit up to the surface of the backyard is covered with boxes and broken furniture. I strain to see into the darkness, the toasty warmth of the hot water heater radiating behind me. I see crates marked "Turpentine," and then, with a jolt, I discover a cracked and empty coffin tossed in the shambles.

At least I hope the black matte coffin covered in spider webs is empty.

Holy shit! Is Sam right?

I want to run or scream. But I am tired of giving in to the shitty hand fate keeps dealing me. As I stare at the coffin, a lump forms in my throat. I bite my lip until a small trickle of blood escapes my mouth. I am standing my ground. More like I am paralyzed where I stand.

I break free and stuff the dirty laundry in the front load washing machine without taking an eye off the casket. My hands tremble as I add the Tide. I pay no mind to the settings and turn it on. Then I let my legs carry me the hell out of that dank and freaky basement.

Back in my room, I pick up the pencil and page through the journal, looking for Beverly's description of the Angel of Death. Again and again, I read the name Samael. I thought the whole thing might be a joke. Now, I can't be so sure.

Was Beverly really involved with Death or a man she associated with death? Is Samael Death's name?

What I initially thought of as a spooky fantasy is becoming a real-life macabre affair between Beverly and an Angel of Death. I run a finger along the line of text where Beverly describes Samael. I start a rough sketch.

Beverly's description is of a handsome young man in a black suit. She describes him as pale with enormous, dark, sleepy eyes, sculpted eyebrows, and a prominent nose. He has a strong jaw and is an eloquent speaker. His speech is pressured but soft. His lips are pink and tucked between his facial hair, a thin mustache and goatee.

With pencil smudges up and down my forearm, I finish my composite drawing. I feel like a true crime detective. I fancy my efforts and gaze at the image before me. This is my best work.

I imagine the man in my drawing younger and without facial hair. Then, I recognize Sam in the picture.

Is Sam this man's great-grandson? Is Sam a Wade?

I am baffled. After studying my sketch, I get up and paste the picture into my disintegrating collage. Most likely, the drawing will be consumed by rot. Like everything else in this house. This is just as well, as I feel compelled to hide the sinister image.

Why did I draw him so meanly?

The washing machine chimes. It lifts through the stillness of the house. I have to flip the laundry. I make a careful descent with a small load of my clothes. When I start the dryer, I stand rigid before it and keenly survey the rest of the basement. I want more proof than a broken-down casket. Maybe Sam is exaggerating things. I need to know if he has been truthful about this place. I am more than a little curious.

Challenging the inexorable horror emanating from the basement is the only way to conquer my fear of this house. One of the storage room doors stands slightly ajar. I watch the opening as I cross to retrieve the knife under the stairs. Then I slowly tiptoe towards the door and peek through the crack, but things are too dark to see. I take a deep breath, put all my weight into it, and open the heavy wood door. It makes a deep groan and scrape like something rising from the deep, coming to the surface to breathe. The lone, naked light bulb behind me gives up a meager shaft of light. Suddenly, I can make out the outline of a concrete slab.

Gradually, with my eyes adjusting, I shuffle inside. I keep my back against the door then the wall as I slink along the room's perimeter. The chilled and damp wall saturates my black *Labyrinth* t-shirt. It is one of my favorites. Deep down, I always get a tickle when I watch David Bowie dance in his codpiece. This isn't visible in the graphic of my t-shirt, which is a collage of Bowie's face in a sea of Muppets, but it always comes to mind when I wear it. The cold, wet wall pricks tiny holes in the back of my t-shirt, ruining it.

The slab of one bed for the dead warbles and turns into twelve slabs in a blink as my eyes adjust to the low light. For reasons I know not, I continue to walk with my right arm stretched out in front of me, and in my left hand, I clutch the knife. I silence the little voice telling me to turn back.

I run my right hand along the wall, stumbling into the corner of the room. With my extended right arm, I find a low-slung shelf chiseled into the wall. Here, I discover another book. Would it be as telling as Beverly's journal?

I put the knife on the shelf and grab the large, black leather-bound book with a blank cover. It looks like an oversized bible. My hands wander over the spine and bulk of the soft, worn leather. I'm curious what secrets this book may hold. If I could only see well enough to read. I crack the book open to anywhere as beginnings and endings didn't matter much in this house.

A slight glow pours out of the pages, wanting to be read, and my eyes rapidly adjust. I discover a long list of names and dates, page after page. It's a ledger of the deceased in a room for the dead, the long-gone dead resting in the cemetery of my yard.

The dead can't hurt you. Abby is dead, and she is good.

I understand that this house has many secrets. Without a doubt, though, there is something more to this ledger. Upon deeper inspection, the ledger also has a recipe for the dead. But this recipe is for body preparation for burial.

After draining the blood, enter the femoral artery with an injection of turpentine, lavender oil, chamomile oil, and vermilion dye. This produces superior results to the messy soaking of the body in arsenic. And the oil of lavender has a better aroma.

I taste the rising bile in my throat and force it back down. *Where the hell am I living?*

Abruptly, the room is crowded—breathless bodies take shape on the slabs. Bodies being drained of their blood. I eye the small rivers of blood pooling in the grooves of the tables. These weren't just grooves; these were funnels, run-offs that spilled the blood into buckets at the corner of the slabs. One bucket overflows, creating a puddle. The room smells of pennies, and I have a metallic tang in my mouth. I spit and huddle against the back wall lined with hooks and leather aprons. On the floor are black rubber galoshes.

The dead moan. I turn back toward the cherished bodies waiting to be placed in the ground. I also view the bodies that would be discarded in a mass grave without care. Some people would have afterlives, and other people just became corpses. They were mere shells of humanity showing the first signs of rot, and their souls were hunted by Death.

Death inches in, a nightmarish shadow moving from out of the corners to drink from body to body. Death has lurked in the dark corners, sniffing and swallowing the essence of decomposition that permeates the walls of these chambers. Death clambers to drink deep of the souls housed inside the feeble frames of man, woman, or child. But Death does not move on. He does not transport these lost souls; he sucks the corpses dry and satisfies himself. Advanced stages of rot are readily seen, and those unfortunate beings waiting to be whisked to an afterlife are relieved of their last hopes by Death. The room's darkness blisters with Death's lust, creating a claustrophobic enclosure packed with the ghastly history of the room.

Suddenly, I am torn from the safety of a witness to an active participant; I find myself wearing a heavy leather apron streaked with blood. I get a whiff of piney licorice from the presence of turpentine on my hands. This astringent smell is covered with a repulsive, cloying, coppery blood odor followed by a hint of lavender. The weak scent of lavender does nothing to make the stench stand down, and I find it increasingly hard to breathe. Then another wave of putrescence and nausea marries to create something pungent and sweet, like rotting meat marinating in cheap perfume. I start gagging. This is no place for the living. The basement belongs to the dead.

I drop the ledger. The thin paper leaves swish and hush as they fall to the floor, and the book splays, buckles, and bends. I grab the knife, run to my room, and slam the door. With my back pressing against the door, I eye the room suspiciously. I hide the knife under my mattress. I don't think a knife can hurt a ghost, but I want it near me just the same. I am mentally crowded and vulnerable. A million thoughts beat about my brain. The stale smell of cigarettes has become a welcome stink in my room.

Are the cigarettes back?

I pat about my body, wondering when I'd taken the apron off.

Was any of that real?

Then I look down at my beloved vegan combat boots. They are rimmed and caked in blood.

I boldly step into the catch-all room opposite my bedroom. Mustering my dwindling strength, I rifle through a remaining pile of boxes under the veil of darkness in the room of things forgotten. I fumble and search for my favorite picture of Abby and me. I need to see it and hold it. I have been trying to keep my memories of Abby at arm's length. But now, remembering seems like the most important thing, the only thing. I want to remember the way things were.

Eventually, I find the photo and rip it from the Disney princess-themed scrapbook Mom had made for us in an earlier time, in a happier time. We were happy in this photo. We'd colored our hair with a Kool-Aid mix. Abby's hair came out as a faded pink, and mine was a pale purple. Abby's smile had gaps from missing teeth, making her a picture of a hockey player more than a little girl.

I feel my blood searing through my veins. A flash of fire burning from the inside out, but it won't take my life. Death does not show that kind of mercy. It leaves you behind, suffocating and on fire. It is the raw feeling of grief.

The pain of being separated from you, Abby, is physical and profound. It's consuming me.

I take the photo as mine and return to my room, where I tuck the picture away with the prayer card from Abby's funeral and the knife. I momentarily linger over Abby's toothless smile, then set the bed to rights.

I want to do it all again, and I don't want to do any of it without you.

Chapter 22
To Tell the Tooth

2021

Anna

THE PHOTO OF TOOTHLESS Abby reminds me of her on the day she died. She had lost her front left tooth that day and told me she hoped to get $2.00 for it from the tooth fairy. I now wonder if Abby ever had a chance to put her tooth under her pillow the day she died. Did she tuck it under her pink pillow before selling surplus cookies with her troop? Had it been in her pocket at the time of the accident? I have no idea.

***

In the chaos of the accident, I forgot to pass on the information about Abby's two-dollar hopes to Mom. Not that it mattered anymore. When I thought of it again days later, I snuck into Abby's room and looked under her pillow. It was a clandestine mission, as Mom had practically taken up residence in Abby's room since she died. I took my chance when Mom was called away to begrudgingly accept the steady flow of casseroles and condolences. A worn five-dollar bill was folded in half under the pillow.

It made me feel better to see it, and childishly, I wondered if it had been the act of my parents or the tooth fairy. I wanted it to be from the tooth fairy. If that could be true, then fairy tales and happy endings could be true, too. Then, an idea wormed its way into my heart. A selfish thought that quickly justified itself. I swallowed hard and ran from the room. I threw myself across my bed and screamed into my pillow as I tried not to think of the five-dollar bill. None of it mattered anymore, but somehow, it mattered more than anything.

I returned to Abby's room when Mom was taking a rare shower. It had been a week since my last visit to the eerily vacated room that was Abby's. I could still smell her between the sheets when I lifted the pillow in my left hand, squishing the pink kitty flannel pillowcase tight in my sweaty fist. I didn't need to exercise such force, but I couldn't help it. All of me was tense. The temptation held me, and I chewed my lips, deep in debate with myself. I scraped the flakes of chapped skin stubbornly sticking to my lips with my teeth. I wounded and tore at the dry bits until my lips stung from the ravaged biting. Lips were much more delicate than nails and not as satisfying to worry. But I'd made up my mind. I would take the five-dollar bill. There was no one to stop me. I never heard of tooth fairy revenge. It had to be the tooth fairy who left the money. Because Mom and Dad knew Abby wasn't coming back. I snatched the five-dollar bill, then set the sheet and comforter to rights and made for my bedroom.

I held my breath as I ran back to my room, opened the closet, and stuffed the money in the front pocket of a hanging pair of blue jeans. I closed the door softly and sighed like a balloon with a small leak.

This five-dollar bill would edge me closer to buying that lipstick I'd been eyeing at Walgreens. I had a half dozen tinted lip balms sanctioned by Mom, but they looked like nothing and were sticky. I'd been eyeing the Revlon Glass Shine Black Cherry lipstick. It was too old for me. It would be a ballsy move. I'd be the first girl at school to sport a bold red lip, like Taylor Swift. It could make me rise through the teen ranks. I may be one of the last girls waiting for her period, but this could be a distraction and deceit from my stalled puberty. It would crown me as the JFK Junior High fashion icon. This lipstick was more than makeup. It was a power play, a declaration of womanhood. If womanhood did not come to me naturally, I'd fake it till I made it.

Whenever Dad used that phrase, he pumped his fists in the air. It usually had something to do with work, and honestly, I thought he looked dumb.

It was a great relief that I no longer had to dwell on the possibility of shoplifting. I didn't want to steal; that was wrong. But I couldn't think of anything else until this opportunity came along. My relief was cut short by knotting nausea in the pit of my stomach as I realized I had just stolen from my dead sister.

Two days later, I returned to Abby's bedroom to replace the five-dollar bill under her pillow. I didn't have the stomach for stealing, lipstick, or junior high—not anymore. I only wanted the one thing I could not have: my sister back. I froze in horror when I lifted her pillow; there was a new crisp five-dollar bill in its place. I dropped the money. It feathered softly to the floor.

Either the tooth fairy was real, or my parents knew. I didn't know if the replacement money was a mercy or silent judgment. In any case, someone knew I was a rotten person.

Sleep was elusive that night. I tossed and turned. Georgie was knocked out of bed. I tried to sleep, but the gnawing emptiness yawned wide inside me. And Dad's snoring in the next room was not helping. Mom, usually zonked by insomnia and wired with caffeine, slept soundly for the second night in a row. Undone with fatigue. The noises of Mom's late-night movements roaming the house were eerily missing. I took it as a cue to wander.

I left Georgie on the floor, tucked halfway under the bed, and left my room. The house was so dark and empty that there weren't even any signs of Enoch. I made a quick stop to liberate the flashlight from the utility drawer in the kitchen. Then, I decided to make a glass of chocolate milk to go. I used five large squirts of Hershey's syrup, but I had filled the glass too high and had to drink a few deep gulps to make it safer to carry.

The feeble light in my left hand only extended one foot before me. I crept through the foyer on my way to the closet when I was caught out by the full moon beaming in through the large picture window in the fancy living room, the room only to be used on holidays and when guests came over. I hadn't been in there since the "after-party" of Abby's funeral. No one called it that, but it sure did seem the case to me.

I paused in front of the coat closet and tried to recall if this door creaked. Nope. No memories of that, but it had always been a favored hiding spot for Abby. Abby had been too young to realize her "favorite" hiding spots were not good hiding spots. I tucked the flashlight under my arm and opened the closet.

I hoped to find Abby hiding there, but I did not, of course. The knowledge that Abby was gone did not fight my instinct to search for her. On the floor, under the winter coats, was a pile of photo albums smelling of faded plastic, befitting the contents of faded memories. I closed myself inside the closet and reached for the thick floral print album on top of the neat stack on a dusty floor. Upon opening this plastic preservation, a flood of emotions was illuminated by my flashlight. Abby's face was smiling up at me, perched over the enormous pumpkin before it was carved into a jack-o-lantern. We had fought over whether the pumpkin should have a scary or silly face. Dad had made us compromise. The result was an appearance of indigestion. I was just out of focus, pouting. I felt stupid.

I turned the pages, smiling and silently crying while looking at Abby. The Navy wool pea coat that had belonged to Great-Great-Grandpa William, whom I had never met, hung above my head and brushed against my forehead. It was itchy but not a deterrent. I had always found the coat to be a bulk of forgotten memories. It was menacing; thus, the closet had never been one of my favorite hiding spots. I didn't understand why we kept the bulky, heavy coat. It didn't fit anyone, and Dad could hardly remember the man. Tonight, I was beginning to understand the unformed whispers of the past were what we all would be reduced to. It was precisely why this common thread of fleeting life was being held onto in both the coat and the stacks of photo albums. And it was why I sat on a pile of albums in this closet with chocolate milk I didn't even like, but it had been Abby's favorite.

I was cramped inside this closet. I shoved a second tower of photo albums to the left to give myself room to stretch out and knocked over the chocolate milk. I hefted the tower of photos even further back to keep them out of the way of the spill. Only the album I had been looking at was dripping with chocolate milk. I took off my pajama top and used it to sop up the spilled milk, which I was literally crying over. I dried everything, including my tears.

I walked through the house with a chocolate milk-stained tank top. I placed the dirty glass in the sink and the flashlight in the utility drawer. Entering my room, finally tired, I shoved my wet pajama top into my wicker laundry hamper and climbed back into bed.

The next night, I went out wandering without the chocolate milk. When I opened the closet, the floor was empty of photo albums and recently Swiffered. The fragrance hung in the air like a heavy accusation.

***

I wonder if Abby's ghost will return to me again. And I ponder how I can bring her ghost back, even if she was a bit spooky looking, all dead and everything. Then I have an idea; I read ahead a few pages from where I had left off in the journal. The journal reads my mind and flips quickly to another blank page that fills with text. The words appear with the usual accompaniment of soft swishing sounds like an invisible pen moving deftly across the page. It is a summoning spell with a sketch of a pentacle. Perhaps I can conjure Abby after all. I rummage about the tokens in the room for a good drawing instrument.

I grab the dwindling pencil. It isn't going to cut it. It will not mark the floor. Then I spy a permanent red Sharpie atop a box. I roll back the round pink rug from Abby's old room that is spread across the floor between the foot of my bed, the chifforobe, and the closet. I eye the space and take another quick study of the sketch in the journal. Then, I draw a large freehand pentacle: a circle with a five-point star inside. It is, more or less, just like the picture. I lean back and shift from side to side, eyeing my work. Not perfectly round, but the star's five points touch the circle, even if a little unevenly. I hope it will work.

Next, I withdraw the picture of Abby and me from my bed and the funeral card and place them in the center of the pentacle. I sit crisscross applesauce in front of the pentacle. I recite the conjuring spell.

It doesn't work.

Maybe I'm not pronouncing it correctly? Or am I just being foolish?

I re-read the page with the spell. It sounds like something out of a slumber party. The candle. I had forgotten a candle. I snatch the Eucalyptus candle from my closet and place it in the middle of the pentacle. It takes me three tries to strike the match. I am getting better.

With the candle lit, I recite:

"Hear these words. Hear my cry. Spirit from the other side. Come to me. I summon thee. Cross now the great divide."

Then I wait and wait and wait.

More nothing.

I twiddle the cartouche between my fingers and feel foolish to think this spell could be real. However, I refuse to give up on seeing Abby again. I just need some glue. I step aside from the pentacle and focus on the shrine where I have witnessed magic, sinister as it may be. I decide I will need a few more things, and that's how I find myself again on the threshold of the unfinished room. At least there is no sign of the phantom face.

I eye the items I want, judge how quickly I can access them and get back out fast. The glue brush is near enough, but the wallpaper glue has somehow migrated to the middle of the room. I make a plan and jump into action. As I enter the room, I keep watching the window as I fumble around and snatch the glue brush. I go deeper into the room, stepping around the ladder and never taking an eye off the window. I fear seeing a floating head near that window or even a head with a body. It doesn't matter much which one. I don't want to see any of it. I drop to my knees and reach frantically about for the tub of glue with my hands. Finding it, I pick it up, too, and then make a backward jog for the doorway. If there had been a door, I would have slammed it.

Entering my room, I gaze upon the pentacle and the lit candle on my floor. It gives me goosebumps. Instinctively, I want to distance myself from this black magic. I hold back my hair and blow out the candle.

What am I doing? What am I so afraid of? I am trying to conjure up my dead sister, but I'm scared of a ghost in the other room?

I feel a little silly. I move my magic to the closet, paste up the picture of the toothless Abby and me on the top left side of the shrine, and then paste the prayer card on the top right side. My shrine to fashion has devolved into a hodgepodge of creepy glamour and ghosts.

This might be hopeful. I can't help but say a quick prayer:

Please, come back.

As a nail-biter under great stress, I have to get my fingers clean for real. I scrub my goopy fingers and cuticles with a sock instead of a washcloth under the running water in the bathroom sink. The drain slowly chokes down the water, leaving a gritty film in the basin. I turn around for the towel hanging on the wall. Then I see Enoch in the corner, stretched out on his side in an unnatural position, with his eyes bulging wide and mouth open. He lies suspiciously tucked behind the toilet. A cry sticks in my throat. I reach down. He is stiff but not yet cold. His fur remains soft to the touch.

I think I will choke on my cries, but instead, I vomit into the toilet. The yellow bile and bits of carrot mix in with the orange stains that would not be scrubbed or bleached away. I sit in the middle of the small bathroom, cradling my dead cat, rocking, crying, and feeling acutely vulnerable. Enoch is dead, and I think it is all my fault, a supernatural consequence of the spell I tried. A life for a life.

However, when I look at the corner, I see the damn rat poison. Instantly, I grow hot with anger and blame my mother.

"I hate this stupid house. And I hate you," I shout to no one.

When I didn't think I could be any lonelier chasing my sister's ghost, my cat dies.

Chapter 23
Troubled Water

2021

Anna

I CRY UNTIL MY face is red and blotchy. Then, I wrap up Enoch in one of my favorite dresses. I plan to place him in the chifforobe to keep him safe.

Safe from what? I don't know.

I throw out a few shoes from the floor of the chifforobe and make room for him there. Sitting in a jumble of stinky tennis shoes and ballet flats with crushed heels, I cry all over again. All my frustration and confusion since Abby died comes rolling back to the surface like a tsunami. I do not have the strength to bury my raging emotions. Eventually, the tears are somewhat therapeutic, like they are being wiped away by a gentle hand. A small fragment of my pain has just been siphoned off, like it is being eaten.

Wiping my face on my sleeve, leaving snot marks behind, I suddenly want my mom. I doubt she could comfort me, but I want her anyway. I pick up the journal on my way out of the room. I can't say why, but I feel obligated to protect it, to keep it with me. I don't want to miss what the journal might say, especially now. Besides, whenever I leave something alone in this house, it turns to shit.

I enter my parents' bedroom and find Mom asleep. Even curled up in repose, I can see the dark circles under her eyes and her cheeks sinking in. She is old beyond her years. She is actively aging at a supernatural rate.

Heck, she even looks older than Grandma.

I had never really stopped to witness Mom's grief and the toll it was taking on her physically, not really. Selfishly, I only considered how Abby's death impacted me and how my parent's grief and anger affected me. It's been all about me.

In shame, I back away from my parents' bedroom door and step into the mint-green bathroom with the journal. I shut the door and turn the heavy deadbolt. This is an odd lock for a bathroom. Someone must have feared being seen naked or on the toilet.

I open the faucet and place the stopper in the tub, adjusting the water temperature with one hand while splashing around with the other. I love the pressure and sound of rushing water. It blocks out the rest of the world and soothes my mind. But I detest the orange ring in the tub.

Has Mom been using the right cleanser?

I see scratches from Mom's extreme efforts on the porcelain, but a pale orange ring remains. I dump all of Mr. Bubble's contents into the running water to hide the relentless stain. I always wanted to do that, to pour the whole Mr. Bubble bottle into the streaming water, but I always had to share with my sister. The tub fills with bubbles, mounds of bubbles that mask the ugly discoloration.

I strip out of my clothes and look at myself in the mirror, turning this way and that. I have a built-in distraction from grief: puberty. It gives me a go-to escapism. I cup my developing breasts, wondering if a corset or bustier would make me look busty or shine a glaring spotlight on my small boobs. I wonder how big they will be someday. They are little buds, and the heavy gold cartouche hangs low between them. But even the diversion of puberty has its limits. My face puckers and pinches with hot tears over thoughts of Enoch.

Is this what I look like when I cry? My classmates saw me looking like this? Jesus.

I turn my face away and step into the steaming water, surrendering myself to the heat, sinking back into the dingy porcelain tub to chillax. I recline until my head rests on the curved lip at one end and my toes touch the other end. The hot water turns my flesh pink.

I will take Enoch to the cemetery tomorrow and give him a proper burial. Maybe Sam will be there. I hope he'll be there. I'd like his help. I fantasize about crying on his shoulder; that way, he can hold me and not witness my ugly cry.

The sound of rushing water drowns out the sound of my tears. The bubbles overflow and I turn the faucet off. I reach for a razor perched precariously on the tub ledge and roll the handle between my finger and thumb. I have never shaved before. My blonde leg hair is light enough so one could hardly see it, but it is plentiful. I lather my right calf and gently rake the razor from ankle to knee. Nothing. I do this three more times before I press hard enough to remove the hair from my leg. Under the caress of my fingers, the naked, slippery feeling of my legs wows me. Now I am more like the ladies in my shrine.

I put the razor back, confident Mom won't notice. Then I grab the towel I had left balled up on the floor, dry my hands, and carefully reach for the journal. I flip through the journal. Some parts are dated and boring, but other passages speak directly to me. I believe this to be true partly because the journal describes my bedroom in this house as it once belonged to Beverly. But another part of me feels confident the journal is talking to me rather desperately, pleading for me to solve some mystery.

I read about the romance between Beverly and Samael. Beverly writes in a lovely, swirling script. Could Samael, who supposedly visited Beverly in this house, be real? So far, I have not seen any sign of his gravestone in the cemetery.

I read randomly, skipping blank pages and reading some of the written pages twice. I grow closer to confirming my suspicions, but I want concrete proof. I lean toward the idea that the house may be the real deal: haunted. No doubt, with it being a hospital/waiting room for corpses. And no wonder why Beverly came off a bit odd.

Raised in the realities and ambiance of death, Beverly is comfortable with Death, even in love. This house may indeed be haunted by Beverly and Samael.

How romantic, sort of.

I search for details in the beautiful penmanship. I come across a page filled with the word "psychopomp" written repeatedly. At the bottom of the page, I read a note:

He is a psychopomp who conducts souls to the other world. But he is mine.

I suddenly realize I need Samael if I ever hope to have a chance to speak with Abby.

But how? Samael, clearly older than Beverly, must be

dead, too. What makes him so unique? Was he a man or more?

I fling the journal. It slides across the hexagonal tiled floor, hitting the wide scuffed baseboard. I am tired of death. Death, death, death everywhere.

How can anyone breathe in these conditions?

I slip under the water and lavish bubbles to escape. This house teems with the dead. The house has claimed Enoch and seems in hot pursuit of my mom.

Am I next?

Under the hot water, holding my breath, I attempt to mentally separate from the rest of the house, seeking freedom from the hallmarks of death. Exhausted with sorrow and anger, I want to wash it all away. My little life has become so lonely. I scream, but no one will hear me under the water—or so I think.

I stay submerged, waiting for the last moment before needing to rise and take a deep breath. This sensation of desperately needing to breathe helps clear my mind, but then a heavy weight presses down on me. It holds me under, reaching inside me, groping between my heart and throat. Burning lungs fight against the lack of oxygen and the pressure of two hands pushing down my shoulders, pinning me to the bottom of the tub.

I open my eyes, and through watery vision, I make out the dark outline of someone blurred. This person holds me underwater with a rigid, unforgiving clamp. Their fingers pinch into my slippery flesh as I struggle. I scream, and a folly of bubbles escape my mouth. A rushing, pounding drum fills my ears, and the sound of breaking water sustains the moan of bending metal.

This horrific melody of death by drowning climaxes as I make my final reach, thrashing my arms. I try to grasp the person but cannot get a grip. I kick my legs, flailing. One foot catches the beaded chain of the rubber stopper and rips the plug from the bottom of the tub. The would-be murderer escapes in a flash, streaking out of the bathroom straight through the locked door.

I pop up from the water, gasping for air. The large tiles on the wall flex like they are choking for air. The tiles buckle and pop. They fall from the wall, splashing and crashing into the draining tub. I try to catch and press them back into place, but there are too many. The wall behind the tiles has turned black with decay.

I scramble, slip while climbing out of the tub, and fall on the towel. Wet and crying and too frightened to stay in the bathroom, I dash to my mom's room across the hall, leaving a trail of little puddles on the hardwood floor.

I climb into my parents' bed and curl up in my towel, creating a damp indentation in the space vacated by my dad. I spoon Mom while softly crying. I turn my face into the pillow to block the growing smell of putrefaction.

Mom does not wake to any of this commotion. She is deep in a supernatural sleep and hot with a fever. A burning slumber wraps her up in her grief like an oversized sweater. From the look of death on her face, her fevered dream gives her a sinking comfort. I understand she is slipping away, but I don't know how to wake her. All the noise I muster does nothing. My screams rise to the rafters, making no impact on her. My touch is pointless, but I shake her, bordering on violence, and call to her all the same.

I am sure I live in a haunted house and wonder if I am the ghost.

I don't want to, but I know I have to retrieve the journal from the dreadful bathroom. It is the only way to find answers about this house. Surprisingly, when I reach the bathroom, it has returned to its usual dingy self. The tiles are on the wall, and the tub is dry, like nothing happened. There goes my proof of a haunted house. Perhaps I am just mad.

I skulk in the doorway armed with a spatula, slapping it about like the worst swordplay, trying to snag the journal. It remains out of reach, and I feel silly. From my hallway reconnaissance and spatula swashbuckling, I determine the bathroom has no evil remnants, so I step inside. Pausing in front of the mirror, I am horrified to see purple indentations in my flesh; I clearly make out the finger marks bruising my shoulders. It is evidence of a run-in with something from the other side. With the journal in hand, I dart from the bathroom.

I breathe a little easier once I get dressed. I select a pair of shorts and a t-shirt from the pile of slightly dirty clothes on the floor. Despite all the laundry I've been reluctantly doing, I still have plenty of dirty clothes to wear. Besides, it seems pointless to try to remain clean in this place. And it's absurd to put on any PJs because I might need to bolt from this house any second.

Dressed and ready for something, I am slowly comforted by Georgie and my room. Something about this one room in the house convinces me I'm not alone—in a good way. Because, well, much of the house makes me feel like I'm not alone, but this room doesn't bog me down with evil intentions lurking in corners, save for my bedroom closet.

Was Beverly trying to comfort me? Or had Beverly been the one who tried to drown me in the bathtub? Maybe she wants us out of the house.

When I get hungry, I bravely go downstairs again to check on Mom and scrounge some food. Mom hasn't changed. I don't know if this is good or bad. I brush the hair from her face and am crushed by her cadaverous look. I blame her for leaving me alone like this in the house, for Enoch's death, and for being unable to get past her grief for Abby.

Why can't she remember she has another daughter, a living daughter?

I visit the kitchen and grab a box of Twinkies and a bottle of A&W Root Beer for dinner. A&W was Abby's favorite. It's not Cherry Coke, but it is soda.

It might be best to go ahead and grab breakfast, too. Once again, I shuttle the Lucky Charms upstairs to my stockpile of junk food. Settling in with a Twinkie in one hand, I read more from the journal. Every word brings forth sympathy for Beverly's plight.

My family wants me to get outside and meet people my age. But people my own age are boring. I have all I want here with Samael. However, I cannot tell my family about Samael, not since they blamed him for my mother's passing when I was born. He has been with me all that time. For decades before I was born, he had waited to be seen by someone other than those lingering on death's doorstep.

As an angel, he should not have let himself get so attached to humanity. For all that, being an Angel of Death does not make one immune to the beauty of humanity. Instead, it drew Samael to the tangible and spiritual union with humans. He longed to be more than a spiritual being on this plane. Samael wanted all the experiences, loves, and losses that come with being human and make the human soul so delectably divine.

Samael had become lazy for decades before my birth, staying at the Wade House, an easy place to snatch souls. He loved our way of life. Our home was like a memorial to him; he basked in the glory and ritual we humans brought to death. But then Death started stealing souls for himself. And instead of ferrying souls to Heaven or Hell, Samael ate the dead.

After this passage, after everything, it becomes clear to me that Samael is a supernatural being, a real Angel of Death. And his usurpation of souls corrupted his angelic state. He is a rogue Angel of Death snuffing out the eternal hereafter where he should have just stayed the natural course. His greatest sin is devouring souls instead of escorting them to the afterlife. Over time, he surges with his gluttony, finding an unexpected companion in Beverly.

The journal reveals that Beverly saw him as a boy in a dark corner waiting to play while still a child. As she grew older, he took up residence in the closet of her room, ever watchful. This way, he could be near and observe her between his feedings. Beverly called on him more and more. Samael discovered himself besotted with Beverly and her ability to engage and communicate with him. They spent long hours talking, both inquisitive of the other's experiences.

Beverly's relationship with Samael from childhood to her forties was threatened when the Wade House was shuttered. Beverly knew nothing else but death, and Samael realized he would have to move on and resume the original intent and purpose of his existence. Both loathed saying goodbye, and deemed themselves cursed by their circumstances. While Beverly wanted to stay with Death, she didn't want to die. Frantically, she searched for a way to keep him with her.

Beverly recounted how she dug through the old books on the gloriously hand-carved yew bookshelf on the second-floor landing. She never did remember anyone reading those books. They were dusty, the titles were worn from their spines, and the bindings and covers were held on by a thread. Through her harried readings, Beverly soon discovered each book contained some aspect of Death from cultures worldwide. It was a necromancer's library, complete with grotesque carvings of monsters conjoined in a twisted display of debauchery on the top and along the edges of the bookcase that Grandpa had carved. She pored over every book, looking for a way to save her Angel of Death, to bind him to her. In her hectic readings, Beverly discovered a book on Egyptology and a book on Exorcism. From there, she painstakingly crafted a binding spell.

Chapter 24
Playing with Death

2021

Anna

I AM STALLING. I must go downstairs and check on Mom again, but I am frozen by fear. I fear Mom being dead, the fear of Death lurking in the corners, and the fear for my own life. I lie perfectly still, wrapped in the rainbow blanket liberated from one of the boxes. While Mom's old hand-knitted blanket is wrapped around me with the comfort of the womb, it is ineffective as any real protection. With the blanket over my head, I hide from the reality of monsters. I hope the childlike strategy of pulling blankets over one's head is a viable fortress to escape all the scary things.

In this prone position, with my left arm growing numb pinned under my body, I can see through the little spaces between the stitches. I don't want to move. I don't want to join a life that is unfair at best and horrific at worst, caught in unrelenting cruelty, revealing a ravenous beast under this roof. I want to hide from everything, even the light of day.

The blanket lets in enough sunlight to make me feel pressured to rise. When I close my right eye, the pinpricks of light are a tiny promise of life, a scattered array of ambiguous light. When I close my left eye, each little bit of light makes a V-shaped pattern of hope. This unwavering light, as small as it is, is the only sense of order in my chaotic world. The little markers of light are scant reminders of a life gone by but maybe a hint of life still to rise.

I toss the blanket off and attempt to climb out of bed. My sheets and blankets cling to my clothes, tugging to keep me couched in place. But I ignore the soft pleas of my bed. I absolutely have to check in on Mom.

I return the Lucky Charms to the kitchen. I've eaten all the Twinkies. Of course, Mom is still sleeping in her bed, but now she's wheezing. That is a new development. She looks like death warmed over, and this doesn't seem a likely reaction to a sprained ankle. I consider that Mom may have a concussion or demonic possession on the sly. I roll up the bamboo blinds to let some sun into the room. The stream of sunshine does nothing to animate Mom's sunken appearance. I observe Mom sleeping and barely breathing. She looks like a Halloween decoration.

I pick up a distinct and pungent odor coming from her. The same smell I hid from earlier, the night before, by burying my face in Dad's flat pillow with yellow stains. Ugly, to be sure, but it released the hint of his Dior cologne and the reassuring musk of his sweat, which always reminds me of freshly sharpened pencils. I hover closer and sniff. I follow the lousy odor to its origin: it is clinging to Mom's back. I lift Mom's flannel shirt at the hem and find a large, dark red, oozing lesion. It's a bedsore as if she were an invalid, having lain in one spot for a lengthy period, immobile and rotting away.

But Mom had only gotten into this bed two days ago. The open, festering wound on Mom's back doesn't make any sense. I certainly don't want to touch it to examine it further. If she doesn't get any better by this afternoon, I will have to go for help. However, I don't want to leave my mom alone in this house for so long. Just thinking about it makes my palms sweat. I believe the house to be haunted because logic is petering out.

But come on, a haunted house? Then again, what better place to bring Abby back.

I want desperately to leave it all, but I can't abandon my mom. I am afraid the house will swallow her alive if left alone. The notion is ridiculous, something out of a horror movie. I am incredulous at the bizarre turn my life has taken.

I nervously step out to the yard, wiping my profusely sweating hands back and forth on the sides of my crumpled jean shorts, trying to dry them. Even with Mom's nagging, I have only washed a meager amount of laundry, so I chose to wear this rumpled pair of jean shorts and my *Stranger Things* t-shirt. The black graphic t-shirt hides stains and allows me to get a lot of wear from the shirt before it looks dirty.

The early morning keeps the heat at bay, but the terrible sun will bear down within an hour or two. I look over my shoulder and into the house. The rising sun makes it impossible to make anything out inside the house, where something lurks and bids me return to the ominous, dark void. I edge a few steps into the yard, still looking back, afraid to take my eyes off the back door swung wide, hungry for my return. It reveals a portal to a murky blackout.

My palms are now making a damp imprint on my denim shorts, which I clutch in my fists. The weight of a loose braid hangs heavy over my shoulder like a lazy snake. Everything about me feels burdensome and sluggish. This house is crushing me, Mom, and everything in it. But I will still return to it again and again. There is nowhere else to go except the cemetery.

I am attracted to isolation with a healthy need for attention. It's a paradox that convinces me that stepping away from Mom and sprinting toward Sam is okay.

This isn't too far from Mom. I will hear a call for help with the back door open.

I make a beeline to where I usually meet Sam. I have become accustomed to this place and no longer watch for snakes in the grass. Sure enough, he is waiting for me.

Thank God I am not alone. I have Sam. But how long did he sit in this field waiting for me to come? Does he ever go home?

I plop down in the tall grass next to him. The dry grass tickles and itches my newly shaved legs. I should have worn pants for walking and lazing about in this wild, parched vegetation to guard against ticks and Lyme disease, but it is entirely too hot. And I want to show off my smooth legs to Sam. For a moment, I stop thinking about the sex appeal of my legs and reflect on Sam's appearance. He always wears the same dark trousers, a button-down white shirt, and a black tie.

Who dresses like this?

Every time I see him, he's dressed like he'd just skipped out on a funeral. I try looking at him askance, but I am about as subtle as a hawker at a carnival. For all his hard looks with puppy dog eyes, I decide he is genuinely dark, even for an Emo guy. But then the guy might be poor and have few fashion options.

"I drew a picture of you," I blurt a sliver of a lie.

"Really? Is it flattering?" he asks.

"It is a good resemblance. Did your family ever live

here once?"

"I'm not a Wade," Sam says.

"Oh," I say.

The conversation falls flat. I had thought he would admit to his relations with the Wade family, but he does not.

What the heck?

We sit together in silence. It engulfs us and holds us bound and stagnant with the lack of the buzz and chirp of nature. Just then, there is a tinkling of bells in the breeze. Sam starts talking softly but fast. His words are dipped in lies, his hair falls forward like a veil, and he knowingly misrepresents the Wade family. At least, it feels like he is spinning a lie.

But why does he want to do that?

"The Wades were not good people, well, some of them. They worked in the trade of death, where they found their opportunity to flourish. They removed gold teeth from corpses and kept them. If the corpse had family, they would stuff the dead's cheeks with sawdust to hide their theft. But Jane and John Does didn't have anyone to notice," Sam says with a wag of his slender finger.

"And, in the case of unclaimed jewelry and valuables, they did not bury these things with the corpses but kept them. 'Finders Keepers,' as they say. Old Mr. Wade stopped listening for the death bells tied to the scarlet strings for those accidentally buried alive. There were too many to listen to, and it didn't make money. Digging up those buried alive just meant bad blood and less money. The whole bell thing was a sham. Besides, with the advent of draining the bodies of their blood, there were no accidental burials anymore. Old Mr. Wade also started burying the recently departed with already buried bodies. The soil, being softer and easier to dig, gave him more land for the dead of the paying families. Nothing was sacred to him."

"Wait, what? What are death bells?" I ask.

"The Wades would tie little silver bells to long scarlet strings. One end of the string was buried with the body. The other end is topside with the bell. That way, if they accidentally buried someone alive, that person could ring for help."

"Are you shittin' me?"

"No, I would not shit on you, Anna," Sam says.

"How do you know all of this?" I say in a whisper, aggressively leaning forward.

I mean, I am boy-crazy but not stupid. And I can't understand how Sam could know all this. Or expect me to buy it.

"Not much goes on out here, especially these days," Sam says. "What else is there to do than learn from history. Besides, you live in the house. Haven't you learned anything?"

"Yeah, that the house is screwed up. Don't think I'm crazy, but I think the house is haunted. I mean, it seems likely with all that death business going on."

I don't want to tell him about the bathroom incident or the journal. I can't understand why I am clamming up, but Sam is shifty. Whatever it is, it isn't enough to keep me away. From under hooded eyes, I note Sam's sly and seductive demeanor.

"Let's talk about something else," I say.

"Like what? Are you tired of death?" Sam asks.

"You have no idea."

"Try me," Sam says.

He looks hungry, and I think I hear a low growl. I spill.

"Before the accident? I told Abby no. I wish I hadn't every day since, but I told her no. Why? Because I was more concerned about being seen with a gaggle of giggling Girl Scouts than being a good sister. The idea of being caught spending time with little girls by a kid from my junior high gave me cold sweats. I was not there when she needed me.

"This wasn't the first time. Ever since I turned thirteen, I'd steadily grown into a monster. A real bitch. I started shutting her out. I was too busy, always too busy. She wanted to play. She wanted to sleep in my room. Abby always knocked on my door, asking me if I wanted to build a snowman, even in July. She thought herself funny and clever, but I thought I had outgrown Disney. I thought I had outgrown Abby.

"That cold, sloppy, wet February evening, life turned on me and shut me out, taking Abby away forever. I learned the hard way she was the only thing that mattered, and then I stuffed those thoughts down and tried to drown myself in my idiotic fashion magazines and lip gloss. But it didn't work. She's all I think about."

I feel buoyant after this deluge of sins. It feels like a confession minus the old, creepy priest.

"I think you sound like a good sister who would do anything to get her sister back," Sam says.

"I would, oh, I would," I say.

A heavy pause settles between us. Then Sam asks, "Have you been in the basement yet?"

The left side of his upper lip curls ever so slightly. It is enticing and bleak. And the awkward silence returns. I want to be near Sam, but I am uncomfortable with his line of questioning. It comes off a little mean-spirited. I can't figure out what he wants, and it frustrates me. Not knowing how to move forward with Sam, I excuse myself.

"I gotta go check on my mom."

Sam isn't ready to let go.

"Please stay," he says. "Let's play a game."

"What kind of game?" I say, suspicious of him.

"I don't know. It's been so long since I've had anyone to play with."

I chew on my thumbnail, and a chip of purple paint flakes off. I don't want to spit in front of Sam, so I swallow the polish chip and glance back at the house.

"I know. How about Touching-Not-Touching," I say. I shiver with my boldness and wonder if he has seen my body's betrayal of my lie.

"Touching-Not-Touching" is a game Abby and I played in the backseat of the car. We pointed at each other, getting closer and closer, but without touching. All while chanting, "I'm not touching you. I'm not touching you." The point was to annoy the piss out of each other. Abby usually won. Abby could be very annoying.

"What is that?" Sam asks.

"We played it at Caitlyn Connor's fourteenth birthday co-ed party," I lie.

I had not been invited to Caitlyn Connor's birthday parties since the eleventh birthday peeing fiasco. Anyway, the invitations were only for girls who had their periods. A "woman's birthday party," Caitlyn had called it. I learned after the fact that two boys had crashed the party. At least, that's what I heard.

"Co-ed?" Sam says.

"You know. Boy and Girl party," I say.

My face blooms with heat, and I touch my cheek, trying to brush away the blush warming my face. I am only used to lying to my parents. I've never lied to a boy before today, but I have never spent this much time alone with a boy before.

Since Abby died, my friends fell away one by one, treating me as if death was contagious. I didn't understand my sudden inflated pariah status. Apparently, fourteen-year-olds have no place for death. My friends, barely teens, did not want the illusion of their youth fractured. They would break free of the safety of their childhood homes in time, soon enough, in their own way, in the sins of their choosing, like sex or drugs. Vices that for a while would make them move as if alive as new budding bodies far out of touch with mortality are inclined to do. Only I knew their thirst for life was a lie.

Thrust to the edge of adolescence with wrecked parents too far from reach to keep me above water, I am tired of treading. I am coming to the conclusion that drowning may be an embraceable option. Certainly, I cannot be expected to navigate a long life without my sister.

"Oh, well, that sounds nice," Sam says, arching one eyebrow.

"Okay, stand up. Alright, we stand about a foot apart with our arms outstretched to the sides. Then, we start ever so slowly to close the gap between us. We have to get as close as possible without touching."

We stand in the tall grass, shuffling closer together.

"How do we know who wins?" Sam says.

"Oh, well, I'm not sure. We are supposed to be competing against other couples," I say.

We are very nearly touching. Sam maneuvers his feet to the outside of mine. I turn my face to look up at him. His chin almost brushes my cheek. If we touch, it is game over, but if we touch, I'll call it a win. We are close enough to kiss.

I wait for him to make a move, but he doesn't. I feel him sniffing me. And it is like he is dragging off the scent of grief and confusion from the top of my head, a heady bouquet of my innocence. I feel open and relieved. I tilt my head further back and lean in for a kiss. But no matter how much I move in, he just hovers before me.

An intense humming emanates between us, just like the first time I donned the necklace. There is a low vibration of energy straining, singing in a resounding note emanating from the cartouche I wear. The necklace clamors to be heard and recognized. The deep hum resonates through my chest.

And then it all collapses at the thought that maybe Sam doesn't like me like that.

My muscles begin to ache. Standing at attention like a living cross, I strain my arms, neck, and back. Sam also struggles to hold position and then reluctantly fades back a few steps, defeated. I am discouraged and confused, bordering on angry. This isn't much of a win. I had anticipated the want inside of him calling me. I tuck my chin to my chest and make a thin line of my lips, fighting back tears of anger. At that moment, I notice his shoes. There is an odd shimmer at the edge of his brogues, a blur to their edges like they aren't real. I chalk the illusion up to the tears in my eyes.

Without a goodbye, I return to the house at a run. I hope to see Mom up and improving, but the sunroom is empty of life. Mom should be up by now.

I go through the lonely kitchen and glance in the bathroom. Mom's bedroom also turns up empty, as well as the front two rooms of the house. I don't think Mom can go upstairs to the second floor with her busted ankle. But I bound up two by two, just the same, to see if Mom might be upstairs. My room is empty, already stifling in the day's growing heat. I hesitate to visit the unfinished space. The room that periodically holds a face in the window.

I take a deep breath and call, "Mom? Mom?" No answer.

I have to look. The room continues to be a mess of DIY products, nothing more. This leaves one place to search. I know I have to go to the basement.

What if she needs me? But why would she go down those stairs again?

At the top of the basement stairs, I hover. I don't want to go down and look for her. Repulsed by the creepy basement, I no longer want to live in this haunted house. This place is crazy.

I've quit better things than this.

I can hear my parents in my head nagging me about how I quit every time things get hard: soccer, gymnastics, and life. It is true. I hold myself up with my celebrity magazines and let the world disappear. This is what I want to do now, but I can't. I have to find my mom. We need each other. But I'm not ready.

I return to my room and reach for the journal on my unmade bed. I need some honest answers about this crazy house. I plan to arm myself with knowledge. I have always been a good student, with a solid A/B+. In my lap, the journal pages turn on their own with seeming purpose.

Suddenly, something reaches out from behind me. I can't see anything but distinctly feel a cold, clammy hand wrap around my shoulder, cross against my tender bruises, making me flinch, and then spider down my arm. The journal slowly closes.

Initially, I dismissed the supernatural in this house as any sane person would. But after my second physical contact with the other world, I am more pressed than ever to manipulate the house into connecting me with Abby. I am ready for something more than a dark illusion.

It is clear I am not alone in this house, and whatever it is has more reach than a mere ghost. I just have to harness it. I bolt from the bed and run down the stairs, escaping from the second floor with the journal. I need to think and read. I sit down in the doorway to my parents' bedroom. I sit with my back to the right door jamb, and my legs are crisscross applesauce. I keep one eye on the basement door and thumb through the pages.

The only sound is my breathing, soft and slow like a lullaby. It belies a calm I haven't known in months. Maybe, with me waiting here, my mom will return. I move back and forth in the book. I don't know what exactly I seek, but the secrets of this house always include a passage about the basement. Evidently, I will have to go all the way downstairs.

Shit.

I relocate to sitting just inside the basement door. I push the door open in one great shove, then perch on the top stair. I am sure something lurks downstairs, and I have the distinct feeling the journal holds the answers to defeating it. If I can only decipher the text, then I can control this thing that possesses this house.

I am determined to conquer my fear and find my mom. I begin paging through the latter half of the journal in a studied and painstakingly slow process. At least my delay over the soft, time-worn pages stalls my inevitable descent into the basement.

I read markings dug so deep into the page that they nearly made a hole. I find Latin text scratched across the pages in thick, bold block letters:

CONFITEOR TIBI ET INVOCO TE ANGELUM MORTIS.

At first, I think it reads: *I know you and rebuke you, Angel of Death.*

But after a moment's reflection I decide it translates to: *I give thanks to you and call upon you, an Angel of Death.*

It is not a rebuke of Death but an invitation.

Another pentacle has been hastily drawn in the pages, and a long list of ingredients runs down the corresponding page. The pentacle is upside down, and each of the five points touches the outer ring. And for some reason, a goat's head is drawn in the middle. The spell calls for a long list of ingredients:

Holy Earth
Fire
Water
Wind
Blood of a Believer
Dying Breath
Paraphernalia of the Dead
Splinter from a Tree of Death

How am I supposed to get these things? And what exactly are they?

I turn the list over in my mind. I have a candle for fire. I can gather a small mound of sacred dirt from the cemetery for the earth, and I will need a knife just to get started. I read the passages in Latin, and the English notes scrawled in the margins.

It is clear that Beverly conducted a similar spell with an Angel of Death once upon a time. This is evident in the earlier part of the journal when Beverly tried to save her family business and keep Death close. However, by the end of the journal, Beverly confesses her ignorance of hieroglyphics and Latin as the cause of Death's corruption. She blames herself and plans another spell, a correction of some sort.

This second spell catches my full and undivided attention. This was how I could unleash Death's grip on this house and my family and then redirect it to resurrect Abby. I know what to do, and thankfully, it doesn't require a trip to the basement. This relief bolsters my spirits. With my pencil, I write at the bottom of the journal page:

Samael, I need you.

I hope this will be enough to summon his attention.

Chapter 25

The Conjuring

2021

Anna

It is time to go shopping for the list of ingredients. I start in the backyard. Standing on the backdoor threshold, I watch for Sam, for any sign of life. Beverly's journal is pressed to my chest under my crossed arms like a chest plate worn by an ancient foot soldier ready for battle.

Am I ready?

The sunset is behind me, and it leaves the yard in a gloaming twilight. It will be hard to spot Sam if he is out there. Besides, I don't know if I want to see him now. I most assuredly don't want to explain myself, yet I would love not to be alone. I dash down the concrete steps and through the yard. The brittle grass scratches rather than tickles as I race through it. The soft swish sound is unappealing and magnifies the stillness of the yard. So, I sing "Would You Like to Swing on a Star" under my breath.

The melody and lyrics are studs of joy in my armor

of fear. I know exactly where I am going. I need dirt from a dead man's grave. The freshest, finest earth in the graveyard belonged to Beverly. I go straight to her and use my fingers to dig. I scoop a generous mound into my pockets. The right pocket has a small hole, which I become aware of as a trickle of earth spills down my leg and into my boot. So, I add several more scoops of earth to the left pocket.

The soil is warm from the day's sun. The graveyard dirt spreads the warmth through my pockets to my thighs, creating a comforting and familiar sensation.

***

I recall Abby's legs pressed against my own as an August sun beat through the car windows. The greenhouse effect easily won the battle with the thin whistle of the Honda CRV's struggling A/C. We leaned into the middle of the car, trying to catch the weak stream of air conditioning as Dad drove us from soccer game to soccer game.

Until I quit and stayed home alone in the cool comfort of our house, already finding life too much of a challenge.

***

I shut the memory down.

The dirt worms deep under my chipped purple fingernails. I remind myself NOT to bite my nails no matter how nerve-racking things get going forward. I pray what I have dug up will be enough. I glance inside Beverly's journal for the next ingredient. The list of ingredients is clear, but this macabre recipe lacks measurements.

How do I know when I have enough?

Besides the Holy Earth, I need the Paraphernalia of Death. I spy a scarlet string and a silver bell listing from a headstone in this decrepit graveyard. Just the thing. I snatch the string and bell from the grave, hoping magic won't be an exact science like baking.

***

I knew too well that precise measurements meant the difference between a tasty batch of cookies and a pile of salty lumps dumped in the trash. It had been a lesson that Abby and I never forgot. Winging a baking recipe led to disaster. Our silly parents tried to eat the salt-ridden cookies by dunking them in milk. When I took a bite, I spat it out in the trash, my face contorted with disgust.

"Why are you eating these?" I asked my parents.

"Because you made them," they answered around mouthfuls of cookies they hadn't choked down yet.

I learned a little about cooking that day and even more about love.

***

I snap out of my memory thanks to the ominous caw of a crow lost under a heavy, dark sky clear of clouds. In its inky expanse, the sky threatens to swallow the earth below. I have to keep moving. I should have brought a flashlight.

The next ingredient calls for a splinter from the tree in the cemetery, a yew tree. When I approach the twisted, dead tree, I recognize the stale odor of the chifforobe. The cat urine scent is even more pungent here. I claw at the bark, breaking what is left of my nails, but I am unable to break off a piece of bark.

At least the moon is out, a smudge of white, whose feeble light cracks the consuming dark that advances on me. It is enough light for me to mark a lone crow with its wings outstretched come to rest on the lowest branch. Spooked, I leave the cemetery without the splinter of wood. The darkness licks at my heels as I race to the back door. Clutching the journal and the sticky memory of a once-happy family, I am determined to restore my family.

"I am going to bring Abby back," I announce to the darkness.

"I'm facing my fears and doing fine," I tell myself, but the words are small and hollow when spoken aloud.

I find myself wishing for Sam as I approach the house. I really would have liked to see him. I would have invited Sam to join me in the house if I'd seen him. However, somehow, I know that this task must be faced alone.

To the right of the house, deep in the shadows, I catch a glimmer. I stop. It is the rotten peach tree, and it's giving off an eerie glow. But it is a tree. I slowly cross over to the peach tree. Its bark is soft and wet, but the tree is not green. I snap off a twig with little effort. It leaves a shimmering residue on my palm. This will have to do for the splinter of wood.

According to the journal, I need to head for the basement to read from the ledger and conjure the cadavers of long ago. I need to capture the breath of a dead man.

I slump, close my eyes, then stand tall and advance to the basement. Of course, the single bulb over the laundry is flickering, threatening to burn out. But I refuse to let darkness stop me. With an arm extended before me, I make my strobe-light descent. If I can't see the creepies, I sure as hell can feel them.

I creep past the litter that I will no longer have to change, the stupid laundry that has taken Mom down, and into the dank death chamber whose secrets will be revealed behind the old oak door.

Keeping my back against the cool, gritty wall, I set

the journal down by my feet on the eroding, sticky floor, and I pick up the ledger. The pages are damp. I cradle the ledger in both arms and nestle it in my stomach with a dull jab in my gut. I flip to the back, where I recognize Beverly's handwriting. I call out the names:

Myrtle Turner, Jacob Israel, Harold Murray, Felix Chappe, and so on.

I lift my head and wait for my eyes to adjust after reading from the ledger. Squinting, I make out one by one the shiver and flicker of corpses from long ago coming forth to the slabs. Gradually, they appear like targets in a shooting gallery. Eleven slabs are filled with the dead in various stages of rot. Bodies of drowning victims bloated and their flesh sloughing off. Bodies of suicide victims with rope burns around their necks. Bodies riddled with bullet holes or disease.

Reluctantly, I eye the cadavers in their advanced state of putrescence. Just wisps of a time gone by, and even in their day, they were made mere scraps that no longer satiated Death's eternal hunger.

I try to push back, but there is nowhere to go. Halted by the crumbling concrete wall, I reach for the ledge to steady myself. My legs are weak, and my free hand brushes across a smooth, cold surface: a hand mirror.

This is an awfully odd spot to worry about one's looks.

Then I realize the hand mirror was a tool of the death keepers. The Wades held this same mirror before the mouths and noses of the dead to ascertain if they were breathing. Their breath would fog the mirror if they were living, even barely. When I raise the looking glass to my face, I expect to see myself and my breath in the mirror, but I see an image of a young woman with long, curly, pale blonde hair piled high on her head. Beverly is superimposed on my own reflection. I am looking at a ghost. The illusion foretells what I could one day look like. I may be a beautiful woman if I can only live that long.

Death himself seeps through the door left ajar, a viscous, unformed entity. As he begins his sloppy feeding on the dead, sucking any remnants of humanity and the divine spark, he begins to take shape. He is still unrecognizable as a fully formed being, but he increases in strength and a jagged mouth forms in the shadow. I scream, but Death pays no heed to my shriek.

All eleven decomposing bodies are memories, their souls wrenched out and fed upon by Death long ago. Forced removal of the soul makes a wet, ripping sound. Death chews and swallows hard, leaving lumps of soul grease running down his pointy chin. These poor souls never realized an afterlife, for they were robbed of their essence. Death devoured their souls without mercy.

I freeze in this echo chamber of feasting by an undeterred Death. I am a spectator inside some horrific memory. Death is not here in real-time. I am visiting a nightmare of how things were once upon a time. I glance back at the image of Beverly in the hand mirror. This is Beverly's memory, summoned by reading the ledger in Beverly's script. If I had read an earlier entry by an earlier Wade, would their memories have escaped the book, too?

Death makes his rounds and settles at the back of the room, gnawing on Harold Murray's bones, sucking the marrow free. I notice one empty slab waiting in the rear and watch as it fills with a whole, untouched specimen. One body with a soul, with hope.

Mom is on the last slab.

She's barely alive, her breaths come haltingly and rattle in her chest. She lies under a gossamer veil that blooms and deflates with inhaling and exhaling. I break free of the memory trance and bolt to her side, yelling, "Mom, Mom! Please wake up!"

The eleven cadavers evaporate with the disturbed and fragile memory ruined.

Just Mom and I are left in the death chamber. I reach under the thin, delicate veil and pull at Mom's arm. I am ready to abandon the spell and run. I will drag Mom from this spot if needed. But when her body refuses to give even an inch, my bravery slips. My confidence wavers. This is all too hard and scary for me to do all alone.

The veil bunches up with my tugging but does not fall free. Under the gossamer shroud, sticky like a spider's web, there glints an impossible light of hope from the gold oval locket with a diamond chip that Mom wears every day. It is the necklace Abby and I picked out for Mother's Day three years back. I reach to open the locket but pull my hand back as if the touch of the locket burns. I am afraid that, instead of finding pictures of me and Abby, there will just be two pictures of Abby. I withdraw my hand, and despite the encumbrance of Mom's stiffening body, I again try to lift her from the slab. I grab her about the shoulders and pull, but she is dead weight.

The veil slips a little more, revealing half of Mom's sinking face. It is the veil between life and death, hanging limp, exposing Mom. She is teetering on the other side. The side of death.

I grab Mom's clammy face in my hands and see a black soot-like substance creeping across her lips, spreading over her chin and down her throat. Under my trembling fingertips, the scaly rash is revealed thick across Mom's cheeks. I scream into Mom's disfigured face, but nothing happens.

My lips pucker. I don't know how to save her. Choking back my tears, I try to heft and haul Mom off the slab once more. But she is too heavy to get off that slab, up the stairs, and out the front door.

Then what? I'd still have to seek help by walking six miles.

I definitely will not be able to drag Mom all that way. I put my head down on Mom's chest and cry. My wet face sticks to the veil, and a hairy spider crawls dangerously close to my cheek. I slap my face and jump back.

I hate spiders. Am I really so easily defeated?

And I remember when spiders defeated me before.

***

"Go back, Abby," I said with a clenched jaw, stumbling in the dark.

In our hurry, we'd left the flashlights behind. We didn't notice while we walked up the lit road that led to the edge of camp and the main road back to the park rangers' cabin. But the teenagers we were trailing had left the trail and headed into the woods. I'd followed them into the thick woods with Abby following me.

There was no path there. The woods were too close fitted with trees like the teeth of a comb, and large rocks cropped up and between the tree roots. This was no place for walking. It forced me to slow my pace since I could hardly see and didn't want to twist an ankle. It allowed Abby time to catch up. The moonlight was a feeble luminescence that came and went with the passing of clouds, making it an unreliable light source. I would walk a few paces and stop, waiting for the moonlight to reappear so I could see where to step. It was hot and muggy. And I was sweating. I'd forgotten my deodorant at home. I'd only started using deodorant earlier in the spring when Ian said I stank after we'd run the presidential mile in gym class. Now, I sniffed my pits while waiting for the moonlight to cut through the clouds. I was not exactly powder fresh.

"Anna, wait," Abby said.

With a little more venom than I intended, I spun around and said, "Go back, Abby!"

"I can't go back. I'm scared. It's dark, and I don't know where I am."

I turned forward once more, ignoring Abby's complaints. I couldn't wait for the moonlight. Those teenagers were getting away.

"Where did they go? I don't see them," I said and climbed up on a large rock between two trees.

"Eek! Oh, yuck. Gross!"

I'd walked into a giant spider web recently spun with its gossamer thread between the trees. I would have seen it in advance if we'd only remembered those flashlights. And I might have admired the intricate weave of the web if I weren't so afraid of all things spidery. But we did not have flashlights. So, I had a face full of the web that had me jumping and dancing as I desperately pulled and brushed the sticky web from my face. I ran my webbed fingers across the bark of a nearby oak. I used my *Labyrinth* t-shirt to wipe my face, and then I carried forward, for I was on a mission.

I was determined to catch up with the teenagers I had seen strolling past our campsite.

But I knew I was going the wrong way when I walked face-first into the spider web. Apparently, the group of teens hadn't come through here, or it would have been their faces covered in a sticky spider web. I gave a good shake to my hair and ran my fingers through it, searching for the web's owner. I came up clean.

Thank God.

"Where did they go?" I mumbled to myself when I heard their laughter, looked through the trees, and saw a cliff face. There they were ten feet up and walking away.

"How did they get up there?"

"I don't know, but I want to go back to the campsite. We could be making s'mores right now, Anna."

"Then go."

"Dad said to stick together. What if they come looking for us? We're supposed to be at the shoreline watching the fireworks."

"Then go already," I said while pulling my hair back into a ponytail. I ran my sweaty hands down David Bowie's face. Climbing the rock face would be an excellent way to shake Abby. Like, I needed a seven-year-old in a *My Little Pony* t-shirt tagging along.

"I'm going up," I said.

"No!" Abby pleaded.

I stepped onto the loose shale rock at the bottom of the cliff face.

I thought it didn't look so high with my head tipped back.

I would ditch Abby before catching up with the gaggle of teenagers. I didn't know what to say when I caught up with those adolescent strangers. But I knew I wanted to check out what they were up to. The first foothold was easy. The rock face was a collection of broken pieces, nooks, and crannies. I thought it would be a piece of cake. Slowly, I grappled with the cliff and inched my way up. My hands skittered across the rock until I found a place to fit my fingertips. My feet alternately dangled and found purchase on the cliff. A rock slipped under my left foot at about six feet up and broke free. It shattered with a clatter below. Abby gasped at the cliff's base.

"Don't do that," I hollered. "You're going to spook me and make me fall."

I shifted my reach to the right, hoping to get a better grip. The rock was brittle and cut into my hand. It was too dark to see the blood, but the wet trickle that ran down my wrist and arm was telling. Plus, the burn of the scrapes and cuts screamed.

"Anna, I don't think you should do that," Abby said.

I ignored her. I was good at that, at least. I'd scuttled two more steps to the right when the rock crumbled under my fingertips. I dug in deeper, but it all kept crumbling away. The rock face was smooth from here on up. There was nothing to grasp.

"I'm stuck!"

My hands dripped with sweat like when I snuck into the living room after Mom and Dad went to bed and watched a horror movie on *Netflix*. Now, it was my horror movie. I was going to fall. I didn't know how to go up or down. The intermittent cloudy moonlight was not helping. I waited for a beam of moonlight to help me see my next move. And I was very sorry that I had been following those stupid teenagers anyway.

Abby was right. We were supposed to be watching fireworks and eating s'mores. I started crying, the tears making little rivulets down my dirty face. My nose was running, and I tried to wipe it on my sleeve. I looked down over my right shoulder. Abby was climbing up.

"What are you doing?"

"I'm coming to get you," Abby said.

"No. You're just going to get stuck like me."

"No, I won't," Abby said.

Abby climbed quickly and further to the right. The rock was craggy on that side, and she made a rapid ascent to the top.

"Put your left foot just underneath you. Kick

around. There is a crevice there. I saw it on my way up," she said.

I kicked around with my foot and found a foothold tucked up underneath me.

"Now, use that to push yourself up and to the right where you can gain a handhold in the craggy part," she said.

Abby's directions allowed me to rise a foot from the top. With an outstretched arm, Abby said, "Take my hand."

"I can't. I'm afraid to let go," I said, clinging to the rock.

"I've got you. You can do this."

"I'm scared." My hands had started sweating again. "I'm going to fall."

"No, you're not. If I can do this, so can you."

With a sigh, I released my right-hand grip on the cliff face and swung my arm up to find Abby's slender arm. Abby grabbed my forearm and pulled.

"Climb," Abby yelled into the night air as fireworks sounded with a series of bangs down the path. "Climb!"

With Abby's feet dug into a small boulder at the top of the cliff, she used her sixty pounds of nothing to pull me up. Together, we scrambled to safety and away from the cliff edge. We lay on our backs in the dust, panting and laughing as we held dirty hands.

"Thank you, Abby."

"What are sisters for?" Abby said. "So, do you want to go find those teenagers?"

"No. I'm done with those stupid teenagers. Let's go watch fireworks and eat s'mores."

We walked hand in hand, laughing down the trail that ended at the shoreline. We saw Mom standing at attention, surveying the crowd, looking for her daughters.

"Girls, where have you been? You're so grubby," Mom said.

"Um, I saw these kids," I started.

"And we followed them because we thought they knew the way. But we got a little lost," Abby cut in.

"Why are you so filthy? Have you been crying?" Mom asked.

"It's sweat," I said. Mom looked incredulous.

"Okay, I tried climbing a rock wall to get a better view of the fireworks and got stuck. And Anna saved me," Abby interjected.

"Oh my God, are you both okay?" Mom asked.

"Yeah, yeah, we're fine," Abby continued.

My mouth dropped. Abby was lying and taking the heat for my stupidity. But she was losing steam in Mom's rapid-fire questions.

"Can we get some s'mores?" I said in an attempt to shut down the line of questioning.

Mom paused, looking between us.

"Yeah, sure. Let's go find your dad."

I reached for Abby's hand once more as we returned to the campsite.

"Thanks, Abby."

Abby squeezed my hand and then let go as she ran to meet Dad walking down the path toward us.

***

I open my eyes. I understand I cannot stay in the basement clinging to Mom forever, any more than I can cling to that night in the woods with Abby. Life persists even if I do not want it to. Life is a series of steps of making contact and letting go. It is time I face Death head-on.

I pick at the veil and tear a bigger opening. It sticks to my fingers like cotton candy. I rip the slit into a gaping hole and feel the rattle of Mom's ribcage with her heavy, shaking sighs. I understand I must be brave or lose everything. I unclasp the locket and hold it gently in my right hand, looking at its soft yellow glow. I stare down my fears and pinch open the locket. Inside are two smiling faces: Abby and me. We have always been there, both of us.

I fasten the locket around my own neck, letting it chime against the cartouche. Together, they will be a talisman to save my family. I recommit myself to the spell and unscrew the top of the Mason jar I claimed from the kitchen on my way to the basement. I place the jar's opening over Mom's nose and mouth. The bloom of a ragged breath fogs the inside of the Mason jar. I screw the top back on quickly. With the glass jar firmly in my grasp, I gaze inside it to see the shallow fog of breath reflecting my mother's dwindling life. That breath is alive, inhaling and exhaling in syncopation with the rise and fall of Mom's chest. It makes me a little queasy.

Once again, a loved one's life falls into my rather incapable hands. I scrunch my eyes and try to will the courage to meet my responsibility. On tiptoe, I lean in to kiss Mom.

"I'm going to get Abby back, and I'm going to save you," I whisper.

Time is slipping away. I must return to my room, the pentacle, and face the unknown.

Chapter 26
Death Takes Its Toll

2021

Anna

I AM CAREFUL WHEN I grab the large pointy knife I have hidden under my mattress. The candle and matches are already on the floor in the center of the red Sharpie pentacle. I refer to the journal for the next steps.

Damn!

I have forgotten the goat drawn in the center of the five-point star. I drop my shoulders, sigh, and pick up the Sharpie. I do my best. Abby was always the better artist. When I finish, the goat's head looks like *My Little Pony* gone wrong with horns. Whatever artistic inspiration I'd channeled while drawing the sketch of Samael evaporated.

I shake it off and decide to move on before losing my nerve. I yank the scarlet string and bell from my back pocket. The silver bell slips from my sweaty grasp and falls to the floor with a chime before it rolls inside the pentacle. Next, I wrap the dirty scarlet ribbon three times around the image I drew of Samael, then I bind that to the Polaroid from the journal. The stranger in the Polaroid has taken on more form as Beverly continues to fade. I can make out his broad shoulders and his cravat.

Who is this guy?

I stare at the unlikely couple in the Polaroid. I faintly feel I might fade away if I am not careful. Being bound to Death looks about as appealing as it sounds. I must convince Samael that I am using the journal's spell to bind a Master (him) to a familiar (me). I must persuade him I can do a better job of the spell than Beverly. I lay the journal down outside the pentacle. I am afraid that placing it inside the pentacle might activate the spell prematurely.

I'm not ready yet. But I don't know what I am waiting for. Kneeling, I place the knife in the star's center along with the candle, the bound images, the twig, the bell, and the jar of a dying breath. It takes half the remaining matches to light the candle due to my shaky hands. They will not stop trembling.

Even though the overhead light diminishes the candle's glow, I am reluctant to turn it off. I am scared and don't think I can read the Latin incantation by candlelight. I don't even know how I plan to do any of this. I haven't felt further from being an adult since I was a little girl hiding under the covers. The bravado of being a teenager corrodes. Hell, I am afraid of my own sister's ghost. I doubt I can do this. I doubt it will work. But I have to try for Mom. So, I rise from the floor and shuffle my feet until I stand outside the pentacle. I read aloud:

"I give thanks to you, and I call upon you, the Angel of Death. The immortal one, who is bound in service to escort the souls of men; the one who is lord over the forty and the nine kinds of serpents in the afterlife. I summon you. Keeper of Souls. Harbinger of Death. Come unto me, might I do your will."

A draft comes from under the closet door, causing the cheap hollow wood to rattle. The draft builds up and swirls around the pentacle, around me. Pelting me with icy, freezing winds. But that is all that happens. I scan over the incantation, growing disheartened. I resolve myself to the dark and turn out the light.

Standing in the flicker of candlelight, I wonder what the problem is.

The knife is the problem. I'd conveniently forgotten to bleed. Scrawled in the corner of the page, Beverly noted that there must be "enough" blood. But she didn't say how much that might be. Beverly is really starting to piss me off. However, Beverly stated it would take the blood of a willing host to summon Death. And it would take more than a finger prick to sufficiently bind Death.

The frigid wind ceases. I want to summon Death, but I had hoped to find a way out of binding Death to me. I wait for divine inspiration.

How do I get out of this alive and untouched by Death, save Mom, and resurrect Abby?

I keep waiting.

Nope, no inspiration. Shit.

Will my plan to alter the incantation be enough? I cringe at the thought of this spell going awry and spinning out of my control, but if that is the only way to save my family, that's precisely what I am prepared to do.

I decide to shake things up. Wielding the knife, I slice up my pillowcase for the bandage I will need shortly. After reading the spell carefully, I step inside the circle of the pentacle, anticipating something bold and formidable. I sense nothing. This emptiness is a feeling I am used to.

Maybe this isn't going to work.

I kneel inside the pentacle, careful not to knock the candle over. The scent of the Eucalyptus barely blocks the gagging stench of rotten cabbage and shit coming from the closet. Blending together, it is ultra disgusting. I will never eat cabbage again. Holding the neck of my shirt pulled over my mouth and nose, I begin a muffled recitation of the Latin resurrection incantation as written by Beverly. At the same time, I sprinkle the sacred dirt from Beverly's grave inside the pentacle.

"Haec dicit Dominus Deus ecce ego aperiam sepulchra vestra et ascendere faciam de monumentis vestris populus meus et adducam vos in terram Israel. Exeunte spiritu, caro adhuc esurit vitae, quam concedam, ad serviendum alteri causae iterum surgas, et corpus tuum vivo prius quam putrescam praebe. Amen."

Then I recite the English translation.

"Thus saith the Lord God: Behold, I will open your graves, and cause you to come up out of your graves, O my people; and I will bring you into the land of Israel. With spirit gone, the flesh still hungers for life that I shall grant. May you rise to serve another cause once more and lend your body to the living before you rot away. Amen."

Despite my two years of Latin, I have no idea what I am saying without the translation. Mr. Smith would be so disappointed. I pick up the knife with my sweaty right hand and run it along my left palm. Nothing. Apparently, it will take a bit of applied pressure to actually cut my hand open.

I'm going to need my hand.

Is this wise?

Maybe I could cut somewhere else, like my thigh? I feel silly and scared. I raise the knife, slippery in my hand, squint, and turn my head to look away as I slice my left palm like an overripe fruit in one digging swipe.

I did it!

"Damn!"

I bring the bloody hand close to my chest. I cry into my bloody palm, accidentally wiping blood across my face, and then squeeze my left hand into a fist. The blood drips into the liquefied candle wax, puddling around the sputtering flame. Next, I rub my bloody palm mixed with my tears on the floor, smearing it across the pentacle. I have completed four more elements of the spell: Holy Earth from the grave, Water from my tears, my own Blood, and the Fire of a candle.

My bloodied hand, poorly bandaged, slips across the lid of the Mason jar, and I haphazardly wrap my half-exposed wound around the lid. Despite the slick blood, I open the Mason jar containing Mom's dying breath. The sound of a feeble sigh is released. I place the now empty jar snugly against the candle. I am running out of room.

There, that's everything. Isn't it?

All is still and quiet.

Great, more of nothing. Why am I playing these games?

The only change has been an increase in the shitty cabbage stench. I pull the neckline of my t-shirt over my nose again. After several silent moments, I grow tired of inhaling my own breath. It makes the bottom of my face hot and moist. These are the perfect conditions for acne. So, I drop the neckline to breathe again. Then I remember what I'm missing. Wind.

Still kneeling inside the pentacle, I blow out the candle. Swallowed in complete and total darkness, I open my mouth to repeat the incantation, at least what I know by heart, but I choke. My mouth opens so wide my jaw aches. A clamor of voices ushers violently from within me. My body rattles, and I speak in tongues. An exodus of evil sounds spills from my quivering body. I lose myself in the darkness and depravity inside this house. Brutal, uncontrollable guilt manifests in a putrid black liquid, spewing from my gaping mouth and splashing across the walls. I am stupefied.

Then, a cracking wood sounds as the rafters splinter, and the closet door simply rolls back to one side to reveal something much more than my closet. My shrine, clothes, and floor are gone. A massive heavy gate swings open under a wrought iron emblem of a serpent eating its tail. This snake wriggles and flexes in the eaves. Unlike the entrance in the graveyard, this one is alive. The snake roils and chokes on its own tail, a warning that Death lies within these gates.

I barely cling to the fringe of reality. I have done this. I have willfully opened this gate to a time and place warped by Death.

Why on earth did I do this?

I wait for Death to rear its ugly head, to issue forth from these gates that have laid hidden in my closet all this time. My heart beats hard in my chest, pounding up into my throat. The cartouche hums to life. Fear dribbles from my shivering body. I've never experienced my heart hammering like this before. I think it will explode. The onslaught of noise from the opening of the gates, which clamor with my hammering heart, makes a symphony to beat out the din of Death. The darkness falls like an ominous silence about the room, absorbing even the faintest hum of the pendant and the overwrought drubbing of my heart.

Is my heart still beating?

I can't hear it. I am not sure if I can feel it. Blood and a snaky ribbon of cotton trail down from my loosely bandaged hand. I wait for Death to come and come he does.

The heavy beat of enormous, glossy, black-feathered wings tinged with a green iridescence fills the air. The pounding is deafening. It marks the arrival of an Angel of Death. But he is not just any Angel of Death. He is Samael—Tempter of Eve, Father of Cain, fallen prince of Heaven, and dark escort of souls. And now, Samael is free of the shackles of corrupt magic.

I clamp my eyes shut and cower, squatting over the pentacle.

Hear no evil. See no evil. Do no evil. Is it too late for that?

I no longer dare watch his ascension. But I can't help but listen. Death comes wearing bells, just as the journal said: *With a clapping din of shivaree.* The sound of wreckage. The very worst of chaos and noisemakers mock my dreams of resurrecting Abby. The clamor makes the permanence of Death be heard. I gag on the sharp, rotten, decay pungent in my nose while it fills my mouth with the flavor of putrefied flesh. I have never felt so insignificant as I do now, and that is saying something. I simply wait for Death to snuff me out.

Then, there is a sudden spark of light, and with an involuntary shudder, I snap my head up, wide-eyed and teary-eyed. The sputtering candle is lit with a black flame that throws grotesque cavorting shadows on the walls. In desperation, I continue to wield the knife, clutched for protection.

Can one even kill an Angel of Death?

The blade blotted with my blood shimmers in the flickering flame in the otherwise complete darkness. The kitchen knife weighs heavy and reassuring, like something substantial in my grasp. Like I might stand a chance. It is my only defense, with all of my frailties laid bare. Within the trembling candlelight, I am a lone morsel in front of the gates of Death. I peer into the abyss that had been my closet and shrine. I squint, trying to make shape or form out of the waves of darkness lapping and leaping in front of me.

I begin to feel a figure starting to surge and form behind me in the center of the room among all my little girl relics. The icy air whips about the bedroom, buffeting my body, making me shiver, spinning me around, and knocking me down as I try in vain to stand. And that's when I see the figure gathering behind me like a pillar of darkness. Its wings extend, spanning the room, brushing the walls. Feathers wedge in cracks in the wall and rain down on me.

Death has a half-finished face with overly large, hooded, and wide-set eyes that swim like black holes. Like a bat, his ears are enlarged and pointy, all the better to detect the despairing screams of humanity. His jet-black hair frames his face perfectly. Slicked back, it hangs to his chin and is neatly tucked behind those ghastly ears.

He has no nose and no mouth. Death is malformed. He's only recently recovered from his involuntary slumber whence he had starved and wasted away. Two flattened nostrils with tiny protrusions bloom in his face as he comes into being. He is obligated to suck in and exhale through his mangled nose. At first, his breath labors like an old man's, but then he chokes like a beast, snorting, smelling the fear wafting off my body. I daresay, he finds the aroma delicious. I stumble backward, half out of the pentacle, and steady my feet to meet the distorted face of Death.

His mouth is still nonexistent, yet I hear the low rumble of his voice inside my head. He pleads for something, but I am too disoriented and shocked to understand what he wants. I do not know what this creature needs, but deep down in my soul, I will not give myself to him. He claws at the flesh where his mouth should be. Muffled, strangled screams come out with grunts through the holes torn in his flesh.

I stoop down and grab at the journal, but in my terror, I knock it out of the pentacle. I swipe at it, not taking my eyes off Death for a second. My hands find the journal and scoop it off the floor. Hastily, I return to the Pentacle with the book in hand.

Is inside the pentacle a safe place? A powerful place?

Beverly had written nothing about this. Frantically, I bob my head between watching Death and searching for an incantation to dispel him. Nothing clearly marks the way. And while I scour the journal, Death tears the flesh from his mouth, leaving a bloody, ragged hole cramped with teeth, each one filed to a razor-sharp point. A perfect Englishman's voice comes forth in a whisper from this deformed entity.

"Finish the spell," he demands.

I look into the face of Death. "I want to see my sister."

"I am not the Angel of Death that took your sister. I am Samael."

I dismiss the implied distinction.

"You made her appear before. Do it again."

"That was an illusion. She is in Heaven. Would you do a spell to rip her from Heaven?"

I grow quiet. I haven't thought about Abby all this time. I selfishly want my sister back to ease my guilt and suffering. It hits like a punch to the gut with a medicine ball, like when I refused to kiss Ian Harold and the next day, he socked me in the stomach with an old medicine ball he'd found in his garage. The wind is knocked out of me. Trying to find my breath and clutching my stomach, I struggle to stay on my feet.

"But I need to talk to her," I whisper.

"You did. You told Abby you were sorry. Let it go."

"I can't."

"But I do not have power over life, to give life. I can only claim life at its fated end. I am an Angel of Death. But if you could find it in your heart to accept me, I can take a breath and live. We could live together, and you would never have to fear living alone again," Samael pleads while whittling thin air with his fingers as if he were weaving a tale. This tell-tale sign of his worry is a momentary lapse in his ploy.

Death sighs as if in resignation and extends a hand. "You had best come with me. You can check in on your sister from time to time. And with me, you never need fear death again," he says. His smile drips with blood. He thinks himself awfully clever. His self-important confidence looms large.

"Because I'll be dead," I say.

"I don't want to kill you. I want to live through you. This spell is to summon me. The completion of the spell binds me to you in this realm. I will walk where you walk. I will shake the dirt of the graveyard from my feet. I will no longer heed the failing bodies' call for my mercy. I will walk beside you always. I will take corporeal form. And for the first time, as I tread this earth, I will be able to indulge in all the goodness and sins man is offered. I want to be with you, Anna. You never need to be alone again," Samael says.

I buckle under confusion and disappointment. My knees hit the floor hard, and I sag. It feels like surrender. It feels like giving up.

I thought a simple reversal of the spell in the journal would undo the binding and banish Death, but only after Abby had been returned to me. Fueled by my guilt, the idea of bringing back Abby is just a deceit. It is just part of Samael's trickery all along.

"Why? Why did Beverly lead me astray?" I whine.

The last words fumble and fall flat with revelation. I look into Death's face as he laughs at me. The truth is revealed. Death has impersonated Beverly all along.

Beverly must have been the last soul he'd eaten.

The blood drips from his widening mouth. The lips curl back. He is ravenous. It has been so long since he fed. It is him, Samael, Death, who has led me astray. I followed his path of crumbs to do his bidding and fulfill his selfish purposes. What's worse, the steady, rich voice with the appealing accent speaks some twisted logic.

Is his way the only way to reach Abby?

"Walk with me, Anna," Samael says. "We can give each other what we want."

So, this is the true Samael.

Beverly's lover and jailer. Beverly's life and demise.

I survey him. Samael makes a dapper man if you ignored the ragged lip. He's dressed in a fine old gray suit, but it deepens and enriches into a fathomless black as I watch him. He flexes his muscles and enjoys his physical form. Under the gleam and disguise of the velvety night, his suit jacket becomes a brocade black on black, something to drown in. Samael's very personage betrays his greed. His simple waistcoat in faded, dirty gray raw silk shimmers with an eerie green, luxurious glow. Then, it bursts into flames in front of my eyes. The waistcoat alone burns. Flames lick Death's body. He rolls his head in exaltation, and the flames are distinguished as the vest blooms into a golden yellow of raw silk with the inevitable snags and snares natural to exquisite silk spun by rare coffin worms. The waistcoat now makes a stunning tailored fit with gold skull coin buttons like the ferry money for an Egyptian soul. And a bulging pocket presumably holds a deathwatch predestined to tell the time to reap all souls if only Samael would listen.

The entirety of his suit begs for the caress of young hands to feed Samael's vanity. Of course, Samael is a fine figure of a man with impeccable clothes when well-fed. His shoes are long, pointy-toed, silver-tipped, and made of fine human leather. Death does like to pamper himself in luxury. These imposing shoes are misleading in which direction they wish to go and disingenuous in their cleanliness. For if Death were to step on me and crush me at this very moment, I'd surely see the shit-streaked soles of his feet.

Samael somehow manages to appear humble, albeit cadaverous, with his unfinished face. As I stand in awe, the buttons shine and wink at me, and the journal heeds their call. The pages of the journal are flipping frantically and falling out. They swarm about the room in a whirlwind pumped by the bellows of darkness that had been the closet.

I drop the book.

While I am impressed and tempted by Samael, I notice the suit frays at the ends. I do not know from where I gain my boldness, but I focus on Samael's face.

Well, what he has of a face.

He grins viciously with his wreckage of a mouth.

I continue my stern gaze upon Samael. I will not flinch.

His voice is more profound than the boy in the yard, but there is no mistaking the eyes, cheekbones, and handsome face that drew me into his confidence. Stalled and silent in my recognition of Sam, I am inclined to be complicit in his unspoken wishes. Deep inside, a part of me yearns for him.

Death in love with himself drones on, thrilled to have an audience once again. He has been all alone since Beverly's death. There is nothing more to eat here, and he cannot leave. Not until we arrived, oozing with grief to feed him.

While Samael pleads his case, I use the time to figure a way out of this trap. I will not be the next Beverly.

I find my voice, albeit shaky. "So, you are Samael? I've read a lot about you."

"Oh, yes? Would you like to learn more?"

"What more?" I ask, trying to sound unimpressed.

"Haven't you figured it out? I am your mysterious boy, Sam. I am a rather dashing young man, no?"

I feign a flirtatious surprise. All those hours in the mirror, flirting with myself, are about to be tested.

This thing really is my Sam. This is just my luck.

Finally, this house's pieces and mysteries come together. Sam is Samael. Beverly was never Beverly. The journal, the rat, the pendant, this house's rot, the bathroom...

Oh My God! The bathroom! He tried to drown me!

And Mom, he was responsible for her decay, too. He'd been nibbling on her all along. It was all Samael.

Death had needed my help. "Sam" had dug in, clawed at me, and tried to find new ways to encourage my journey, to bring me closer to his wishes. He had led me to find the proper ritual to bind me to him and free him of the house, finally ridding him of its previous owners, the Wades.

My skin prickles with goosebumps as Death's full deceit dawns on me. I feel so stupid.

I am but a vehicle to an end. Death's nightmare of the consumption of souls depends on me. And now, on the verge of victory, Samael grows impatient and restless. This process, this seduction of me to unbind him from the house, is taking too long. His hunger swells, and he has never learned how to contain it.

Samael flickers and glitches; then, in his place,

stands Sam, looking more and more like a cross between Timothée Chalamet and Finn Wolfhard. He has dangerous cheekbones and tousled tresses. Decked out in stylish all-black clothes, there is a decidedly sexy glow about him that has never been fully realized in the yard. This time, he is fashioned as if on his way to a dashing coming-out party—or my funeral. He is an illusion, hand-crafted by Death and fueled by my imagination, my glaring shrine. Samael has been inside my head since I got here.

"Anna, it's me, Sam. I want to be with you. No one can understand you like I do. Please, don't send me away. I only want to be near you."

He smiles, but not his smile; it is Samael's. Malformed and perverted, it drips with blood, and flesh snags between his shark-like teeth. I open my mouth to protest, but nary a sound comes out. I clutch my throat, trying to choke out a sound. When Sam fades and Samael reappears, my fear rips a full-throttle scream from my throat, and it pitches about the room in an anguished echo.

"You need not scream. I can hear you. But by all means, scream if you must. I enjoy the strained vocalization of fear and surrender," Death says.

Samael shifts his weight and gazes into his cuticles' little glowing crescent moons; he breathes upon them and brushes them against his vest. Then Death peers into my eyes.

"But let us think of more pleasant things. When you complete the binding, I can present in whichever form you prefer," he hisses.

I think about Sam. How he understood me because he was Death.

But what does Death understand about living?

And who could say I wouldn't be restrained to this

house with Death like Beverly? Again, Death prances in my head like he is playing in a toy shop.

"It won't be like it was with Beverly," he says. "She tried to keep me against my will and mucked up the spell. But now I am here to help you, to help us."

He flickers and shrinks to Sam's figure once more. Sam reaches out a hand and brushes his fingers against my blood-stained cheek. I've never felt his touch before, and I melt more than just a little. He shudders with the taste of innocence simmering and wafting from my flesh. He licks the air with his forked tongue—the better to taste me.

I am befuddled. I stare into Sam's eyes and am captivated by the same sinking annihilation I have come to recognize in my mom's eyes.

My mom.

"Free my mom. Free my mom, and I'll do it." My voice is shaky at first, but slowly it is restored with a false sense of bravado.

Sam straightens up and once again becomes Samael. He gives a flourish with his left hand. I am left to assume Mom is all right, but I don't really know.

How can I trust Samael? He is filled with pride and disobedience.

Samael flexes his strength and his image ripples. This Angel of Death grows stronger right before my eyes.

"Anna, I am bound by my word," Samael says.

"So, you say."

Is this true?

All through the journal, Beverly warned that Samael had been corrupted in the binding. But what did that mean? What had been Beverly's words? What had been Samael's manipulation?

I don't know what to believe. I struggle with Death's

seduction. I feel something brush against my bloody hand. It tickles and itches, but I see nothing. I grasp at the air like trying to catch a firefly until I grab hold of the unseen. It is a hand, and it squeezes my hand. I can't see or hear her, but I know it is her. Abby. I can feel the little bones in her hand, her sticky fingers entwined with my own bloody fingers. Nothing needs to be said. Forgiveness is unnecessary, but I feel compelled to ask it anyway.

"I love you, Abby. I'm sorry. Can you forgive me?" I whisper.

Snot drips over my lips.

"The pain of being separated from you is physical and deep, and it's consuming me. We were supposed to live together," I say softly.

Against Death's prancing and incessant talking, I realize I cannot get Abby back, yet I know I am not alone. Death is an illusion. My and Abby's love is forever. I think of my stupid shrine. It is a lie. I look at Death; he is trying so hard to be perfect and is rambling on, paying no mind to me and my revelation.

"I need you to hear me. I am lost. I don't know who I am without you," I continue to whisper under the currents of Samael's tirade and coercion.

My confession cracks me open and breaks my heart. I shiver, my hands shaking blood from my fingertips in a spray over the pentacle. There is plenty of blood now. Samael moves and speaks as if he or I were underwater. All this time, I continue to hold the essence of Abby near. It is a warmth that suffuses my soul. It fills me up inside and spills over. Her spirit stays with me. It is a part of me.

I am Abby's sister; that is all I need to be.

When I hear Samael's words again, I know I don't want any of his dealings. Even though Abby's hand fades from my grasp, I embrace all the broken parts of life, my family, and myself. I will put myself back together again.

I face Samael and say, "This is not real. You are not real."

"What do you know of reality?" Samael sneers.

"Most people change their clothes, not their body. And in real life, people have bad haircuts."

Samael laughs. "I am too perfect? Is that it?"

"Almost, but you have the worst breath. You smell and taste like shit."

Samael is too desperate for my cooperation to be offended.

"My dear Anna. I don't want to hurt you. I just want to be with you, a part of you. You'll never have to be alone again. Isn't that what you want?"

This stymies me, for this is precisely what I want. But I don't want it from him. I close my eyes and try to will Abby back, once more, to feel her hand in mine. I still don't know how to define myself without my little sister.

But I owe it to Abby to try. To live. It's still my turn in life.

And then I realize I am not without. I wish I still held Abby's hand, our palms pressed against each other. But I don't. Abby is in Heaven, yet somehow, she is still here, a part of me forever. It is up to me to save our mom and myself from this clown of Death.

I sway as I wipe my bloody palm across my shirt. I really need to properly bind the wound. The loss of blood is gross and is making me light-headed. The unwashed, worn, crackled graphic of my *Stranger Things* t-shirt feels rough against my open wound. This showdown with Samael feels awfully painful and sticky for something that isn't real.

"Please, Anna, don't dismiss me like you have Abby. Don't send me away. You'll be left alone with your pictures in a magazine. All alone. But with me, we can be together forever. Don't be like the commoners. Don't become food for my appetite. Because, in the end, Death consumes everything. But you, I'm offering you immortality. Help me step out of the shadows, and you'll never fear the end again."

I have wanted so badly to go back in time to save Abby and apologize to Abby that I failed to realize the memories of Abby had kept us together all along.

I squirm. My skin itches. Something bigger than me is stretching and fighting to crawl to the surface and out of my skin.

This thing is my own doing. I have struggled with the loss and attempted to fill the hole inside me with ghosts and magic. The loneliness grew with every moment. But I am not alone. All of my faded and vivid memories and my undying love for my sister are still mine. They are a warm comfort like Abby's embrace. Every sticky memory is a part of me, like when Abby got gum in my hair.

I bathe in the gummed-up, messy memories of Abby. I will hold on to each and every one.

The memories have always been mine. At first, these memories threatened to drown me. They swelled and overwhelmed. I thought it would be the death of me, but now they calm and come forth softly. They will nurture my soul if only I will let them.

I stand frail and nearly finished in front of Samael. But the memories are building inside. I am returning to life, recalling every giggle and tear that will fortify me against this corrupt Angel of Death.

I exhale deeply. My head aches, and my hand continues to bleed. I wipe my hand across the filthy t-shirt again. There is no time for bandages. I am weak and weary. Despite my aching body, my love for Abby is the calm in the eye of the storm. I go back to my big sister place deep inside. I extend my arms and raise my palms. There is only one way forward, and that is letting go.

I will not let go of Abby; I will always carry Abby with me. It is letting go of the guilt I'd been harboring. Guilt that has done nothing but bind me to fear and Death. Abby is so much more than her death. I need to remember that. In this way, going back is moving forward.

Remembering Abby is a blessing, not a curse. I have to allow Abby the space to move on. I have to allow that even though Abby is in Heaven, she is always with me at the same time. I don't need Death to find Abby. Abby has been here all along.

A small light emanates from me. With well-placed defiance, I lay the journal open to the revised spell on the floor inside the pentacle. I have all the tools I need. It is time. I have no idea what will happen, but I believe I can send Samael back.

I stand inside the pentacle with the flickering flame, the blood, the journal, and the bonded images. I brush away a wispy piece of hair from my messy, loose braid and sweep it across my dirty face. The hair tickles a pimple on my chin, but I can only be bothered to register this on the slightest level. There is more to a girl than her appearance. I'd just learned this the hard way. I push past my superficial thoughts and train my mind on the way out. I wriggle my big toe inside the pentacle like taking water's temperature. Then I kneel in my own blood.

What are blood-stained knees at this point?

"You have become an enemy of God. Let me show you how despicable you are," I say as I launch boldly into the prayer I had memorized off Abby's funeral prayer card. The devotion to St. Michael.

"I call upon Saint Michael the Archangel to defend me in battle. Be my protection against the wickedness and snares of the Devil; May God rebuke him, I humbly pray; And do thou, O Prince of the Heavenly Host, by the power of God, thrust into hell Satan and all evil spirits who wander through the world for the ruin of souls. Amen."

From where I know not, the incantation in Latin comes in a surge, and I wrap my bloody fist around the cartouche. The holy word is like honey on my tongue.

"Sancte Michael Archangele, defende nos in proelio, contra nequitiam et insidias diaboli esto praesidium. Imperet illi Deus, supplices deprecamur: tuque, Princeps militiae caelestis, in virtute Dei, in infernum detrude satanam aliosque spiritus malignos, qui ad perditionem animarum pervagantur in mundo. Amen."

Death fumbles the moment, dumbfounded at my courage and knowledge. He had been careful to feed me a load of bullshit through the journal to confuse me.

Next, I recite the incantation in reverse. I reach inside a pocket and sprinkle the remaining graveyard dirt from Beverly's grave over the pentacle. I brush my now slow-bleeding palm across the tears on my face like war paint. My fear turns to righteous rage, and it mounts until I teem with the urge to exert power, to take control. I am tired of Death dictating the terms of my existence.

I want to wrest control of my life from the icy claws of Death that dug its talons so deeply into my flesh. I reluctantly realized I could not and did not need to save my sister. Abby is in Heaven. But like hell will I let Death have Mom. I am terrified, but I will not give up and quit.

My outburst of anger provides the distance I need from Sam/Samael to take over my feelings and do what

I need to do. I am unsure how to proceed, but I will just have to wing it. It is time to be brave.

I grab the charms of both necklaces around my neck and squeeze them in my bloodied hand. I forge them in love and prayer, casting off corruption and creating tools of God. I call forth Saint Michael the Archangel again.

A burst of flame shoots from the floor to the ceiling, scorching both black.

I recite the Latin incantation for St. Michael three times over.

"Mundo in pervagantur animarum perditionem ad qui, malignos spiritus aliosque satanam detrude infernum in Dei, virtute in, caelestis militiae Princeps, tuque: deprecamur supplices, Deus illi Imperet. Praesidium esto diaboli insidias et nequitiam contra, proelio in nos defende, Archangele Michael Sancte. Amen."

A dark wind begins to suck from the room into the vortex that had once been my closet. Samael catches me with a stormy eye. Still clutching the talisman and locket, I interchange my chant between both Latin and English.

"Mortifer, Samael, mors tua, vita mea."

"Bringer of death, Samael, your death, MY LIFE."

A sudden, violent, thunderous shudder shakes the house. A whirlwind wraps around the room. Samael cries out in a beastly shriek. I tighten my bloody grasp around the charms. The rough edges of the cartouche gouge my tender open wound before yielding in my hand. I continued to chant the spell in reverse.

Samael's senses are sealed up in an overgrown lump of rotten flesh. He is torn from the floorboards and spun upside down as I recite the spell backward. Samael is ripped to pieces until just the sound of his anger persists. Then his screams and final remnants are sucked back through the gates of Death.

Once Samael is greedily devoured, the iron and gunmetal gates slam closed. There is the sound of a terrific collapse; space and time shut up and reseal the back wall of the closet, dressed in shredded images of the shrine of celebrities. Clothes hang in the closet, in piles on the floor, and are tossed all about the room.

I drop everything and run from the room, calling for Mom. Only one slab is occupied in the basement: Mom's. Her breathing has stabilized.

Mom opens her eyes. I rip the veil from her, lay my head on Mom's chest, and sob as I listen to her steady heartbeat. Eventually, with a teary and blood-marked face, I raise myself and help Mom up the stairs and out of the house.

I wait with Mom on the sidewalk. When she is coherent, I blow my nose in the hem of my ruined t-shirt, then walk six miles to call for an ambulance.

Chapter 27
Where Death Goes to Die

2021

Anna

MOM IS IN THE hospital for a week to stabilize before the doctors will release her. Their diagnosis is fatigue, dehydration, and accidental poisoning due to black mold in the decrepit house. I would have laughed at this, but I am too tired. No one would have believed me that the proper diagnoses was demonic possession and being eaten alive by Death.

During this time, Dad races home from his business trip and stays at Mom's side until he can return to the Wade House and retrieve our belongings. He doesn't believe me about the haunted house. And Mom can't remember anything after the fall. It is apparent to Dad that we had a big scare, and it was all his fault for leaving us. We will never say this to him, and he will never forgive himself. He only now begins to understand the burden of guilt that we carried over Abby's Death. But what good does guilt do? It is too much, too late. Dad exorcises his guilt by vacating that piece of shit house.

I surprise him with my request to return to the house with him. It solidifies his opinion that the place, while creepy and inconvenient with its outdated construction, must be guilty of being nothing more than old and derelict. Angry with himself regarding this whole mess, he clutches the car's steering wheel with excessive pressure. Too late, he realizes he never should have moved us out there nor left me alone with my deeply grieving Mom. But at the time, his own sorrow consumed him and blinded him from realizing his running from the pain was just running away from his family.

His plan now is swift packing. But my intention is to investigate. Under the guise that I will be packing, I, oh, so slowly ascend the stairs. This feat is only possible in daylight with Dad's presence on the first floor.

I hold my breath and step into the room where I confronted Death. I exhale when I realize the scorch marks on the floor and ceiling have vanished. The wallpaper still clings to the walls in scraps. But my clothes are hung neatly in the closet. My shoes are set out carefully on the closet floor next to the tufted velvet pillow.

The shrine is gone. There isn't a hint of glossy magazine photos or glue. I step inside the closet and run my hands over the walls. The hole in the back wall is nowhere to be found. I rummage through the clothes and dive into the farthest corner of the closet. Everything is solid, albeit a little chilled.

I step back out of the closet and look at the chifforobe. No matter how I push the burnished wood, the door won't budge. I even resort to twisting and turning the stuck key, but this is useless. Whatever secrets and magic this massive piece of furniture contained; they are no longer mine to behold.

I am reluctant to take my eyes off the monstrous piece of furniture. Gradually, I return to the stack of empty boxes and wonder what became of Enoch. I can't bury him if I can't open the chifforobe where I left him. Chalk up one more loss to this haunted house.

I start packing, but I keep glancing around the room for signs of my struggle with Death. Dad sings "Would You Like to Swing on a Star" downstairs. I smile and hum along while I strip my bed, stuffing the bed linens into a box. I stumble on Georgie, lying on his side on the floor, sticking out from under the bed. I reach under the bed and swipe my arm outstretched to snag Georgie from the dark. I am struck with shame for leaving him behind in this house, alone. But Georgie seems to be no worse for the time apart. I wonder if I'll ever lead a guilt-free life. Lovingly, I tuck Georgie in a box.

When I turn back to the bare mattress, I see the journal. It is perfectly intact. Like Samael's waistcoat, the raw silk golden cover blooms bold and vibrant. The pages, still filled with beautiful penmanship, no longer hold secrets. Every page in Beverly's script fails to list or mention any spells.

How could harm sprout from these benign words?

The last page is new. In fresh ink, in a tall, slanted script, I read:

Dear Anna, I shall miss you, but I will see you on the other side. - Samael

I had nearly fallen for the journal's guise of innocence. But now, I instinctively know this book must be removed and destroyed. Gone is the duct tape that I had used to secure the spine. Yet, I find the bindings of this book are indestructible. I yank on the covers and tear at the pages. It all results in nothing.

I notice the slim book of matches in the corner of my room. With trembling fingers, I strike match after match. The journal will not light. Breathless and embittered, I begin to fear the book.

Then inspiration strikes. I will hide the book where no one will ever find it. I make my way back to the graveyard. I start digging with my hands in the loose dirt of Beverly's grave. I dig until my fingers cramp and my cuticles are filled with dirt. The shallow hole will have to make do. I place the journal in the hole.

I grasp the pendant around my neck, which is no longer a cartouche with hieroglyphics. In my confrontation with Samael and my call to St. Michael, the pendant transformed into a simple, slender gold bar marked only in Latin with St. Michael's prayer.

The inscription reads: *Sancte Michael salva me et ligabis Samael ad inferna. Amen.*

I mumble the words while twirling the little holy weapon of war. Although my hands are plenty grubby, no smudge, no fingerprint marks it.

"St. Michael, save me and bind Samael to the grave. Amen."

Tangled in my dirty fingers, this holy relic, no longer a botched attempt at Egyptian magic, has been transformed into a sacred talisman forged in the words of Heaven. I realize the necklace is needed to guard against evil and stand watch in this cemetery. I tuck the sacred amulet in the hole with the journal.

I should say something. Something to keep these items buried. I pull out Abby's funerary prayer card from my back pocket and recite the prayer:

"St. Michael be our defense against the wickedness and snares of the Devil. May God rebuke him, we humbly pray, and do thou, O Prince of the heavenly hosts, by the power of God, thrust into hell Satan and all the evil spirits, who prowl about the world seeking the ruin of souls. Amen."

I place the funerary card in the hole with the talisman and the journal. It is difficult to let go of the religious relics, but I am brave. I am in awe to realize I had the power and grace of Abby's love with me all along. I had been foolish and let my anger over losing Abby and my desire to bring Abby back cloud my judgment.

I finally finish with the tools of Death and safely bury the book under the protection of St. Michael the Archangel. It is concluded. I return to the house a little dirty and begin hauling boxes down to the car.

"We'll let the movers get the rest," Dad says.

"Why don't we just get all new stuff," I say, shuffling my feet, more than a little leery of everything that ever touched this house.

Everything but Georgie. He gets tucked safely in the way back of the Honda CRV. I wanted to carry him in my lap but didn't want to look like a baby. So, Georgie sits in the box on top of the wrinkled bed linens. He peers out the back window, watching the house grow smaller as we drive away.

I braid my hair with my nervous and dirty fingers. I look forward to finding a place where I belong.

Epilogue

2023

PERRY STEVENS MADE A profit off the Wade House. He sold it to a developer who razed the house and graveyard to build a vast complex of apartments and condos. The digging unearthed an old journal filthy with dirt and a few other relics. But these things were quickly lost in construction and scattered over the Wade property, misplaced in the far-back foundations of the luxury condos.

The complex launched a troubled existence with its construction. Three men died in the building of the modern housing. The lives lost called out to the Angel of Death. One of the original tenants committed suicide. In another building, there was a murder. The development was well on its way to a haunted reputation. People intrigued by the mysteries and stories flocked to the place.

After the first year of unrelenting horrors, prices dropped. A young man lucky enough to take advantage of these falling rates moved swiftly in despite the rumors. For the first time, he could taste luxury on his budget. He entered his apartment after stopping by the mailbox.

He did not walk alone. Something walked beside him, an unseen thing in the form of a man in a beautiful suit that screamed well-worn wealth. A thing thrilled to be called upon by murder, suicide, and multiple deaths. This creature fashioned after man was an other-worldly thing wanting a haunt. With the gory smile of a monster ready to feast, he walked inside number forty-two, following closely behind the living, young man.

"DID YOU THINK I, SAMAEL, AN ANGEL OF DEATH, COULD BE SO EASILY UNDONE?"